BETSY
and the
CIRCUS

D0104328

YEARLING BOOKS/YOUNG YEARLINGS/YEARLING CLASSICS are designed especially to entertain and enlighten young people. Patricia Reilly Giff, consultant to this series, received the bachelor's degree from Marymount College. She holds the master's degree in history from St. John's University, and a Professional Diploma in Reading from Hofstra University. She was a teacher and reading consultant for many years, and is the author of numerous books for young readers.

For a complete listing of all Yearling titles, write to
Dell Readers Service, P.O. Box 1045,
South Holland, IL 60473.

BETSY
and the
CIRCUS

Written and illustrated by
CAROLYN HAYWOOD

A Yearling Book

Published by
Dell Publishing
a division of
Bantam Doubleday Dell Publishing Group, Inc.
666 Fifth Avenue
New York, New York 10103

ISBN: 0-440-40197-6

Reprinted by arrangement with William Morrow and
Company, Inc.

Printed in the United States of America

July 1989

10 9 8 7 6 5 4 3 2 1

CWO

To JOSEPHINE
with love from one of the tulips
in her enormous garden

CONTENTS

BETSY
and the
CIRCUS

CHAPTER 1
Mr. Kilpatrick's Birthday

It was a stormy March morning. Betsy was only half awake but she could hear the rain beating against the windowpane. She turned over and buried her face in the pillow. Then she heard Mother's voice calling her.

"Betsy!" she called. "Time to get up!" Mother opened the door. "Come along, dear," she said. "It's a very stormy day."

"Mmm!" said Betsy, opening her eyes. "All right, Mother."

1

Mother closed the door and Betsy sat up. She stared at the window. It looked as though a great giant were throwing tubfuls of water at the window. The wind rattled the glass panes and whistled around the corner of the house.

Betsy got out of bed and went to the window. She looked down into the yard, where in summer Mother had a garden. Now it was a great mud puddle with here and there a dripping bush. The bare branches of the trees blew in the wind.

A car passed, throwing water as high as its windows. It was a bright red car and this reminded Betsy of Mr. Kilpatrick, the policeman, who was the friend of all the children at school. He had been a very special friend of Betsy's ever since she had been in the first grade. Betsy remembered now that today was a very important day. It was Mr. Kilpatrick's birthday and the boys and girls in Betsy's class were having a birthday party for him, a surprise birthday party.

Betsy ran into the bathroom. She was glad she had taken a bath last night. She would be ready in a jiffy. She was in a hurry, for Mr. Kilpatrick's birthday present was not yet wrapped. Betsy had bought it yesterday and she was pleased with it. She felt certain that Mr. Kilpatrick would be pleased too. It was a shiny belt buckle with a design on it that Betsy thought looked just like the badge that Mr. Kilpatrick wore on his coat. The man who had sold it to Betsy said it was made especially for policemen. She had been delighted to find something so perfect for Mr. Kilpatrick.

Betsy ran downstairs as soon as she was dressed. She went into the kitchen where Mother was frying bacon.

"Good morning, Betsy," said her mother.

"Good morning, Mother," said Betsy. "Do you know what?"

"What?" said Mother.

"It's Mr. Kilpatrick's birthday," replied Betsy.

"He certainly picked a wet day," said her mother.

"Doesn't make any difference," said Betsy. "We're having the party indoors at lunchtime. Mr. Kilpatrick doesn't know a thing about it. He'll be surprised, all right."

"Will there be a cake?" Mother asked.

"Of course!" said Betsy, picking up a glass

of orange juice. "Billy Porter is bringing the cake. His mother baked it. Mrs. Porter makes wonderful cake with very gooey icing."

"Come, sit down and eat your breakfast," said her mother, placing on the table a soft-boiled egg with bits of bacon floating around in it.

Betsy sat down and stirred her egg. "Where's Father?" she asked.

"Father left very early today. He took the car," replied Mother.

"Then do I have to walk to school?" Betsy asked.

"I'll ask Mrs. Porter to stop for you," said Mother. "I don't imagine that Billy is walking to school with a birthday cake on a morning like this."

Mother went into the hall to telephone to Mrs. Porter and Betsy ate her breakfast. When Mother returned she said, "Mrs. Porter says she'll be glad to pick you up."

"That's good," said Betsy, as she drank the last drop of cocoa.

As Betsy left the kitchen she said, "Mother, have you any very nice paper that I can use to wrap up Mr. Kilpatrick's birthday present?"

"I'll see," said Mother.

Mother looked in a closet and pulled out some pieces of paper. She put them on the hall table. "This is all I have," she said.

Betsy looked them over. The first one she picked up was a piece of white paper with Santa Claus in his sleigh dashing all over it. "Well, it isn't a Christmas present," said Betsy. "I can't use that."

The next piece was pale blue with the word *Baby* written all over it, in white. "This won't do either," said Betsy. "Mr. Kilpatrick isn't a baby. He's a great big policeman."

Betsy picked up a third sheet. It was pink with pictures of a baby's rattle all over it. "Oh dear!" said Betsy. "More baby stuff."

Underneath was another sheet. It had bright flags on it. "Oh, this is lovely!" cried Betsy. "This is just perfect for Mr. Kilpatrick."

Betsy wrapped up her little parcel and tied it with a piece of red ribbon that still had a Christmas tag hanging from it. Betsy took it off and tied a little card on the ribbon. She had written it the night before. It said *Happy Birthday to Mr. Kilpatrick from Betsy.*

"Did you see what I bought for Mr. Kilpatrick, Mother?" said Betsy.

"No, I didn't, dear," said Mother. "What did you buy for him?"

"Oh, it's wonderful," said Betsy. "It's a belt buckle and it matches his policeman's badge. The man in the store said it was made specially."

"How nice, Betsy!" said Mother. "Weren't you fortunate to find it?"

"I'll unwrap it and show it to you," said Betsy. But just as she was about to untie the ribbon, a horn sounded out front. "Oh, there they are!" Betsy cried, and she put the package into her schoolbag.

Mother opened the front door and called out, "Just a minute," while Betsy took her raincoat out of the closet.

In a minute Betsy was ready with raincoat, rubbers, and umbrella. She picked up her schoolbag and kissed her mother good-by. Mother opened the front door and Betsy dashed out into the pouring rain.

"Hi!" shouted Billy Porter. "Get in the back, Betsy. There isn't room for you in front, because I've got Mr. Kilpatrick's birthday cake here on the seat."

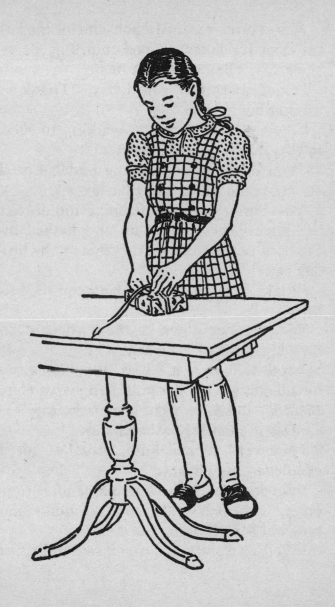

Mrs. Porter reached back and opened the car door for Betsy. "Good morning, Betsy," she said, as Betsy stepped in.

"Good morning," said Betsy. "Thank you for coming for me."

"We couldn't have you walking to school in this rain," said Mrs. Porter.

"You ought to see the big puddles in the streets," said Billy. "Regular lakes."

Mrs. Porter took off the brake and drove up the street. Betsy stood up and looked over the back of the front seat. "Where's the birthday cake?" she asked.

"Right here on the seat between us," said Billy.

Betsy looked down at the cardboard box. "It's big, isn't it?" she said.

"You should see it!" said Billy. "It's a swell birthday cake. It's got pink icing with *Happy Birthday* in white, right across the top."

"Has it candles?" asked Betsy.

"Not yet," replied Billy, "but I've got the candles in my pocket."

"We don't know how many candles to put on it," said Betsy, "because we don't know how old Mr. Kilpatrick is."

"Well, I've got two dozen," said Billy. "You

can't get any more than twenty-four candles on the top of a cake, anyway."

As Betsy sat down on the back seat of the car, Billy shouted, "Oh, boy! Look at this flood ahead. It's like a lake. Look at that car! It's throwing the water as high as the roof."

Billy stood up to look at the big puddle of water. His mother swung the car as far away from the center of the puddle as possible. As she did so, the box with the birthday cake slid across the seat. At the same moment Billy sat down and he sat *kerplunk*, right on the birthday cake.

"Oops!" cried Billy.

Mrs. Porter stopped the car by the curb and Billy got off of the birthday cake. Mrs. Porter covered her face with her hands. "I'm afraid to look," she said. Betsy was leaning over the back of the seat again. She looked down at the smashed box. Billy lifted the lid and looked inside. "I guess I sort of knocked it out of shape," he said.

Mrs. Porter took her hands from her eyes and looked at the cake. It was indeed out of shape. It was broken into a great many pieces and it was very flat in some places. Most of the pink icing was sticking to the inside of the lid. "What a mess!" exclaimed Mrs. Porter.

"I don't know how it happened," said Billy.

"You just sat on it," said his mother.

"Oh, dear!" exclaimed Betsy. "Now Mr. Kilpatrick won't have any birthday cake at his party."

Billy looked as though he were going to cry.

"Now never mind," said his mother. "It was an accident. You didn't mean to smash the cake."

" 'Course I didn't," said Billy, "but there won't be any birthday cake for the party and you can't have a birthday party without a cake."

Mrs. Porter started the car again. "Well, it can't be helped," she said.

When Betsy and Billy walked into school, their faces did not look cheerful. The children were busy piling the presents that they had brought for Mr. Kilpatrick on a big tray. There was a sign Ellen had made that said *Happy Birthday Mr. Kilpatrick.*

When the children saw Billy they called out, "Where's the birthday cake? Did you bring the birthday cake?"

Billy hung his head. "I sat on it," he mumbled.

"What?" cried the children. "What did you say?"

"He sat on it," said Betsy.

"Sat on it!" cried Kenny.

And then the children turned to each other and said, "He sat on it."

"He didn't do it on purpose," said Betsy. "It was an accident."

"Miss Ross," cried Christopher, "now we haven't any birthday cake for Mr. Kilpatrick."

Suddenly, above the voices of the children, the bell sounded for school to begin.

"Take your seats, boys and girls," said Miss Ross. The children went to their seats. There were no happy faces. "Now cheer up!" said Miss Ross. "There will be plenty of ice cream and all of these lovely presents. Mr. Kilpatrick will be delighted."

"But whoever heard of a birthday party without a cake?" said Kenny.

"I don't want to hear anything more about the cake," said Miss Ross. "Billy is sorry, but you can't put a birthday cake together again."

"Miss Ross, what did Mr. Kilpatrick say

when you asked him to come and have ice cream with us?" said Ellen.

"Oh, he said he would be delighted to come," said Miss Ross.

"You don't think he guessed that it was a surprise party for him, do you?" said Christopher.

"I don't think he had any idea of such a thing," said his teacher.

"He would never guess we even know it's his birthday," said Betsy. "I'll bet he doesn't remember that he ever told me. On my birthday I told him it was my birthday and I said, 'When is your birthday, Mr. Kilpatrick?' And he said, 'Oh, I blew in on a windy day in March— the 13th. It's always been my lucky day.'"

"I guess he'll think it's his lucky day when he sees all those presents," said Ellen.

"Come now," said Miss Ross, "we have a lot of work to do before the birthday party. Let's begin our spelling lesson."

The morning seemed very long to the children, but at last it was time for lunch. As they stood in line to go to the lunchroom, Miss Ross said, "Now remember, boys and girls! Return to your classroom as soon as you have finished your lunch."

"We won't forget," said Mary Lou, " 'cause there's going to be ice cream and cake."

"No cake," the boys shouted in sad tones. Billy's face turned bright red.

"Well, there will be ice cream," said Miss Ross.

"And Mr. Kilpatrick," said Betsy. "I hope he doesn't come before we get back."

The children were back in such a short time that Miss Ross, who had stayed in the room, had not finished her sandwich.

"Has he come?" one child after another asked, looking around the room.

"Not yet," said Miss Ross. "And remember! Not a word about his birthday until Betsy brings in the tray with the presents. The tray is in the coatroom. And then I'll bring in the ice cream."

In a few minutes Mr. Kilpatrick stood in the doorway. The big policeman was smiling broadly. In one hand he was holding his hat and in the other a big box.

"Here he is!" the children shouted. "Here's Mr. Kilpatrick!"

"Come in, Mr. Kilpatrick," said Miss Ross.

"Glad to be here," said Mr. Kilpatrick, walking to Miss Ross's desk. There he deposited his hat and the big box. Every eye in the room was on the box.

"I've got a little surprise for you boys and girls," he said, and he began to open the box. "Today happens to be my birthday and"—here he lifted the lid—"Mrs. Kilpatrick, she knew that I was coming up here at lunchtime and she made me a birthday cake."

Mr. Kilpatrick lifted a great big cake out of the box. "I thought I'd like to share it with you boys and girls," he said.

"Oh, boy! That's some cake!" cried Christopher.

It was indeed a handsome cake. It was as fine as the one Billy had sat on, only it had white icing and pink trimmings. The children all crowded around to read what it said on the top. It said *Happy Birthday*.

"Mrs. Kilpatrick didn't have any candles," said Mr. Kilpatrick, "but I told her that didn't make any difference. She couldn't have put them all on, anyway. The cake would have broken down with the weight of 'em."

Billy ran to the coatroom and reached into his coat pocket. When he returned he said, "I've got some candles, Mr. Kilpatrick. I've got twenty-four candles."

"Well, now! What do you know about that!" said Mr. Kilpatrick. "Here, you stick them on."

Billy stepped up to the cake and began poking the candles into the icing.

"Billy sat on his birthday cake," said Kenny.

"He did?" said Mr. Kilpatrick. "Well, I'm mighty glad he didn't sit on mine."

"But he did," several children shouted.

Mr. Kilpatrick looked very surprised and puzzled, but just at that moment Betsy came in with the tray piled high with packages. Miss Ross followed with the ice cream. The children began to sing, "Happy birthday to you." Then they shouted, "Happy birthday, Mr. Kilpatrick!"

Mr. Kilpatrick looked very surprised when Betsy handed him the tray full of packages. "Are these all for me?" he said.

"Yes!" cried the children.

"Well I . . . I . . . just don't know what to say," said Mr. Kilpatrick. "I thought I had a surprise for you and now you have given me the biggest surprise. I guess I can only say thank you. Thank you very much! They look like wonderful presents."

By this time Miss Ross had lit the candles on the cake. Several of the girls were passing the ice cream around.

"Now, Mr. Kilpatrick," said Miss Ross, "you must blow out the candles."

Mr. Kilpatrick gave a mighty blow and out went every candle. Then Miss Ross handed him a knife and he began to cut the cake. The children's mouths were watering by the time they each received a slice. It was delicious cake. Betsy thought it was even better than Mrs. Porter's.

When the bell rang for the afternoon session to begin, Mr. Kilpatrick stood up to go.

"Well, I'm sorry I can't open all of these presents while I'm here," he said, "but I'll open them when I get home. This has been the nicest birthday I ever had."

That evening Mr. Kilpatrick sat at the kitchen table opening his birthday presents. He passed each one to Mrs. Kilpatrick and Mrs. Kilpatrick said, "My! Isn't that a lovely necktie?" "Now what could be nicer than those pencils with your name on them?" "What a beautiful handkerchief—all hand-embroidered!"

When Mr. Kilpatrick opened Betsy's package, he said, "Now just look at that belt buckle!"

Mrs. Kilpatrick looked at it carefully. "There's a lot to that buckle," she said. "It looks something like your badge."

"Does at that," said Mr. Kilpatrick.

"It's even got some letters on it," said Mrs. Kilpatrick. "Words, I think."

Mr. Kilpatrick took the buckle in his hand again. "I believe it has," he said. "But I can't read it."

"Here, take the magnifying glass," said Mrs. Kilpatrick.

Mr. Kilpatrick held the magnifying glass over the buckle. "Well, what do you know about that!" he said.

"What does it say?" asked his wife.

"Sure, it says *Member of the Fire Department*," said Mr. Kilpatrick.

"The fire department!" exclaimed Mrs. Kilpatrick. "Well, they're nice lads in the fire department."

"Sure!" said Mr. Kilpatrick. "It's a nice buckle and nobody ever looks at my belt buckle through a magnifying glass, anyway."

CHAPTER 2

Santhamum Rose and Whitey

Ellen had been Betsy's very best friend ever since they were in the first grade. They always ate in the lunchroom at school together and played together at recess.

Once they had both spent a whole summer on Betsy's grandfather's farm. That was the summer before Star, Betsy's little sister, was born. Ellen had a little sister too. Her name was Linda. She was just a year older than

Star. Linda went to kindergarten, but Star had not yet started to go to school.

Often on Saturdays Ellen and Linda would come to spend the day with Betsy and Star. The two older girls spent hours making paper dolls, while Star and Linda played with Star's toys.

One day at recess Betsy said, "Oh, Ellen! I have something exciting to tell you."

"What is it?" said Ellen.

"We have new beds, Star and I," said Betsy.

"Beds?" said Ellen.

"Yes," replied Betsy. "I have two beds in my room now. Mother says you call them twin beds. And Star has two beds too, only hers are on top of each other. You have to climb up a ladder to get into the top one. They call them bunk beds."

"What are you going to do with so many beds?" Ellen asked.

"Mother says now we can have our friends come and stay overnight. Won't that be fun, Ellen?"

"Oh, yes!" said Ellen.

"I want you to be the very first one to sleep in my twin bed, Ellen," said Betsy, "because you are my best friend."

"Oh, that will be fun," said Ellen. "May I come soon?"

"Yes. Maybe next Saturday," said Betsy. "I'll ask my mother."

When Betsy asked if she could invite Ellen to come the following Saturday and spend the night, Mother said she thought it would be very nice.

"Can Linda come too?" asked Star.

"Of course!" said Mother.

The following morning Betsy said to Ellen, "Mother says I can invite you and Linda to come on Saturday and stay overnight."

"Oh, that's wonderful!" said Ellen. "My mother said I could come if you asked me."

When Linda heard about it she said, "Will we take our nighties in a suitcase?"

"Oh, yes," said Ellen. "Just as though we were going on a trip."

"And our toothbrushes?" said Linda.

"Oh, yes, and our hairbrushes and combs," said Ellen.

"I have to take Whitey and Santhamum Rose, 'cause they always sleep with me," said Linda.

Santhamum Rose was a one-eyed rag doll and Whitey was a squashy rabbit who had lost one ear and whose tail was fastened on with a large safety pin. Santhamum Rose looked out at the world with a stony blue stare. She looked very one-sided. Whitey looked one-sided too, rather more lopsided than Santhamum Rose. They had gone to bed with Linda ever since she was a baby.

"It's just one night," said Ellen. "You don't have to take them for one night."

"Yes, I do," said Linda, " 'cause they're my poor little babies. Santhamum Rose only has one eye and Whitey only has one ear."

Linda had never gone away to stay over-night and she could hardly wait for Saturday to come.

At last Saturday morning arrived. Ellen's mother brought out the smallest suitcase the family owned and put it on a bench in Ellen's room.

"I want to pack my own things," said Linda.

"Very well, you can pack your things while Ellen is at the store," replied her mother, as she took one of Linda's nightgowns out of a drawer. "You'll be a very good girl, won't you, Linda, and not give Star's mother any trouble?"

"Yes, Mummy," said Linda.

"And do what Ellen says," said her mother.

"All right," said Linda, putting her bathrobe into the suitcase. She got her toothbrush out of the bathroom and her comb and brush from the top of her little chest.

Her mother opened the closet. "Here," she said, "you must each take a dress to wear to Sunday School on Sunday morning." Linda took the folded dress from her mother and placed it on top of her bathrobe. Her mother put Ellen's things in a neat pile on the bed.

When Ellen returned from the store she went up to her room. She lifted the lid of the suitcase. It looked like the inside of Noah's ark. There lay Santhamum Rose, her one eye staring up at the ceiling, and Whitey with his safety pin in full view. There was also a toy monkey, a black-and-white panda, a spotted horse, a pink elephant, a black woolly dog, and an Indian doll. On top of the pile lay a small red umbrella.

"Linda!" Ellen cried out. "You can't take all of this stuff!"

Linda came running into the room. "But they're my children," said Linda. "I can't leave my children."

"Well, if you can't leave your children,"

said Ellen, "you had better stay home with them. Where am I going to put my clothes?"

Linda came and lifted her children out of the suitcase, all but Whitey and Santhamum Rose. "I have to take these, 'cause they would miss me most."

"All right," said Ellen. "But not the umbrella."

"Oh, dear!" Linda sighed, as she removed the umbrella. "Everybody takes an umbrella when they go traveling."

Finally the suitcase was packed and closed and Ellen's mother carried it downstairs. About ten o'clock Betsy's mother drove up with Betsy and Star on the front seat of the car. Ellen and Linda were waiting at the front window, with their coats on. When they saw the car, Ellen called out, "Mummy, here they are!" Their mother opened the front door and carried the suitcase out to the car. The children ran ahead.

"Hello!" they called.

"Hello!" Betsy and Star called back.

Linda and Ellen kissed their mother good-by and the two children climbed into the back of the car.

The four little girls played out of doors all

morning. After lunch Star and Linda went upstairs to take naps. There was great excitement over the bunk beds.

"You can have the top one," said Star to Linda.

"Oh," said Linda, "I'm glad. Do I take off my shoes before I go up or afterwards?"

"Oh, before you go up," said Star. "You don't get into bed with your shoes on."

The children laughed while Linda untied her shoes. There was a great deal more laughing after she had climbed up to the top bunk. She had never been so close to a ceiling before. As she looked down she could see the top of every piece of furniture, even the circles that were the tops of the lamp shades, spread out below.

She could see Santhamum Rose and Whitey sitting on a chair. They looked as though they were holding their heads in their laps. To Linda it was a new world, like being up in an airplane and looking down on the earth.

Star and Linda chattered and giggled until Star's mother came to the door and said, "If you children don't quiet down and rest, you can't have a tea party this afternoon." This quieted Star and Linda, for they loved a tea party. Mother closed the door and both of the little girls closed their eyes.

Soon Star fell asleep, but Linda kept opening her eyes and looking at a fly that was walking on the ceiling. She felt that she could almost walk on the ceiling too. Once she stretched her legs up as high as they would go, but her feet were still far from the ceiling. She wished that she could touch it with her toes. She had never had her feet on a ceiling. It would be fun. She tried and tried. She almost stood on the back of her neck, but her legs were too short.

Finally Star woke up. "Linda," she called, "are you awake?"

"Yes," replied Linda. "Can we get up now?"

"Yes," said Star. "Now we can have the tea party."

Linda came down the ladder and the children put on their shoes.

Linda picked up Santhamum Rose and Whitey, and the two little girls went downstairs. They found that Betsy and Ellen had a little table set with Betsy's doll dishes.

"Can Santhamum Rose come to the party?" asked Linda.

"Oh, yes," replied Betsy. "And Whitey, too."

Linda brought her doll and rabbit to the tea table. She sat them side by side on the same chair. Whitey, as usual, leaned his head against Santhamum Rose.

Betsy went to the kitchen and returned with the little teapot and a plate of crackers.

"Is there real tea in that teapot?" asked Linda.

"It's cambric tea," said Star. "We always have cambric tea."

"What's cambric tea?" Linda asked.

"It's hot milk with just a little bit of tea in it," said Betsy.

"And lots of sugar," said Star.

The four children pulled their chairs up to the table. Betsy was pouring the tea into the six cups when her mother came into the room. She was carrying a small chocolate cake covered with chocolate icing. "I made a little cake for you," she said.

"Oh, Mother!" cried Betsy. "This is really a party!"

Ellen passed the cups of tea while Betsy cut the cake. Linda placed Santhamum Rose's cup on the chair, between her legs. Whitey's she placed in front of him.

The children sipped their tea and ate their crackers and cake. Betsy made several trips to the kitchen to fill up the teapot, because it did not hold very much. The cups were so little that Ellen drank ten cups of tea and Betsy drank twelve. Star said she drank fourteen, but Linda said, "No, it was eleven."

"How many did you drink, Linda?" Ellen asked her little sister.

"I don't know," replied Linda. "I just drank."

Santhamum Rose's back was not too strong, and as the tea party progressed she bent farther and farther over her teacup. Whitey slid down lower and lower in the chair.

Finally Linda said, "I'll drink Whitey's tea. He always likes me to drink his tea." Linda drank Whitey's tea and then reached out to straighten up Santhamum Rose. As she did she gave a loud scream. "Oh," she cried, "she's lost her eye!"

Linda jumped out of her chair and picked up her doll. "Oh! Oh!" she cried. "She's lost her eye. Look at her." Linda clutched her doll to her as big tears began to roll down her cheeks.

"It must be on the floor," said Betsy.

"Stop crying, Linda," said Ellen. "We'll find her eye. It must be here."

Ellen and Betsy and Star were soon crawling around on the floor, looking for Santhamum Rose's one blue eye. Linda just sat rocking her doll. Every once in a while she would say, "Have you found it?"

The answer was always no. Then Linda would begin to sniffle again and say, "Poor Santhamum Rose!"

Finally the three children gave up the hunt. Betsy and Ellen began gathering up the dishes. "We have to wash them," said Betsy.

"I'll help," said Star, and she picked up Santhamum Rose's teacup. It was still full of cold tea. She lifted the tiny cup to her lips and drank the tea. Then she looked down into the cup. "Oh, look!" she cried. "There's a blue button in the bottom of this teacup."

Linda came to Star's side and looked into the cup. "That's not a button," she cried. "That's Santhamum Rose's eye!" She picked it out of the cup.

"I think Mother can fasten it back," said Betsy.

"Do you think so?" asked Linda.

"Let's go see," said Betsy.

The children found Betsy's mother sewing in her bedroom. "Mother," said Betsy, "can you fasten this eye on Linda's doll?"

Mother took the doll in her hands. "Of course I can," she said. "I can sew it on."

Betsy and Ellen went off to wash up the tea dishes but Linda and Star stayed to watch Santhamum Rose's eye being put back. When it was securely fastened, Star's mother said, "I believe I have another doll's eye in my button box."

"You have?" said Linda.

Mother went to the closet and brought out

a round tin box. It was filled with all kinds of buttons. With her fingers she poked around among the buttons. Star and Linda bent over the box, watching.

Finally Star's mother said, "There it is!" But when she picked it up she said, "Oh, it isn't a blue one. This is a brown eye."

"Let's see," said Star.

Star and Linda both examined the brown eye. "Maybe there is a blue one," said Linda.

"No, I'm afraid not," said Star's mother. "There was never more than one in the box." She held the brown eye up to Santhamum Rose's face.

"It looks nice," said Star.

"I never heard of anybody with one blue eye and one brown one," said Linda.

"I had a friend when I was a little girl who had one brown eye and one blue one," said Star's mother.

"Didn't she look funny?" said Linda.

"Not at all," replied Mother. "Shall I sew it on? After all, a brown one is better than no eye at all."

"All right," said Linda.

Soon the brown eye was in place. Linda looked at Santhamum Rose for a long time.

Then she said, "You don't have an ear some place for Whitey, do you?"

Betsy heard her and called upstairs, "Oh, Mother! Look in the patch bag. I think I saw one there. You know—it came off the rabbit that I lost on a picnic once."

Her mother went to the closet and brought out a big blue-and-white-checked bag. She emptied it out on the bed and looked through the scraps of dress goods. There was at least a little piece of every dress that Betsy and Star had ever owned. Linda and Star helped to turn all the scraps over until Linda called out, "Is this it?" She held up a long white bunny's ear, lined with red velvet.

"Yes, that's it," said Betsy, coming into the room.

Linda looked at it. "Whitey's ear has pink inside," she said. "This is red."

"But it's an ear," said Star.

"Yes," said Betsy. "I'm sure Whitey would rather have a red ear than no ear at all on that side."

"Pin it on him, please," said Linda, handing the ear to Betsy's mother. Mother pinned it on and everyone looked at Whitey.

"It looks nice from the back," said Star. "Just like a real rabbit."

"All right," said Linda. She handed Whitey over to Betsy's mother and said, "Will you sew it on, please?"

The new ear was fastened to the side of the rabbit's head in a few minutes. Linda said thank-you and carried her children downstairs.

"Isn't it wonderful to have your children all fixed up?" said Star.

"Uh-huh," said Linda, placing them on the little chair again.

Betsy and Ellen began to play jacks on the floor. Star brought out some picture cards. "Come on, Linda," she said, "let's play this game."

"I don't want to play a game," said Linda.

"Now, Linda," said Ellen, "play the game with Star."

"I don't want to," said Linda, and she choked. Then she burst into tears. Suddenly she picked up Santhamum Rose and Whitey and dashed out of the room and up the stairs to Betsy's mother.

"My goodness!" said Mother. "What ever is the matter?"

Linda plopped Santhamum Rose into Mother's lap and cried, "Take it off! Take it off! She doesn't look like Santhamum Rose any more."

In a flash of the scissors the brown eye was off. Linda looked at Santhamum Rose and gave a sigh of relief. Then she handed the rabbit over to Mother. "Whitey says he doesn't like his new ear. He says, 'All that red stuff! It's too hot!' He isn't cumferable."

CHAPTER 3
A Quiet Night

After dinner Betsy's father read a story to Betsy and Star and their two guests and soon it was time to go to bed.

"Would you like to say your prayers right here before you go upstairs?" asked Mother.

The four little girls knelt down in a row beside the couch and said their prayers. Then they said good night and bounded up the stairs. The four pairs of feet sounded like a couple of ponies.

Linda had Whitey and Santhamum Rose under her arm. Betsy and Ellen went into Betsy's room, and Star and Linda went into Star's room. Ellen took Linda's nightgown and bathrobe to her. She found Linda alone. Star was already taking her bath, with Betsy's help.

"Now don't dawdle, Linda," said Ellen. "Get ready for bed. Here's your toothbrush and don't forget to use it."

"Ellen," said Linda, "I wish I could sleep in your room."

"Now don't be silly, Linda," said Ellen. "There's just the bathroom between the two rooms."

"Will the doors be open?" said Linda.

"I don't know," said Ellen. "Maybe."

"But I want them open," said Linda. And she began to cry.

"Now, Linda," said Ellen, "if you're going to act like a baby, I'm going to ask Betsy's father to take you home. Mummy said you weren't to give any trouble."

"All right," said Linda, and she choked back the tears.

As Ellen left the room she said, "Good night, Linda."

"Good night," said Linda. "But I would like the door open."

Linda picked up Santhamum Rose and climbed up the ladder. She placed her doll in the top bunk. Then she came down and carried Whitey up. She plumped him against the pillow. With her bedfellows settled, Linda came down the ladder and began to get undressed. She sat down on the floor and took off one shoe and one sock. Then she pulled the shoestring on the other shoe. It was in a knot. She pulled and she tugged and she picked at the knot, but she could not untie it. Finally she gave it up and took off her clothes. She put on her nightie and her bathrobe and began to look at some picture books.

Before long Star came out of the bathroom. Then Linda heard Betsy calling. "Linda," she called, "you can take your bath now."

"I had a bath this morning," said Linda.

"Well, clean your teeth and wash your face and hands," Ellen called out.

"All right," Linda answered. She washed her face and hands and scrubbed her teeth. Then she went to the door that led into

Betsy's room and called, "Ellen! Ellen! I want you."

"Go to bed, Linda," Ellen called back.

"But I want you," said Linda.

"I'll come after I take my bath," said Ellen.

Linda returned to Star's room. Star had disappeared. She sat down on the floor and began to pick at the knot in her shoestring, but it seemed to be tighter than ever. She got up and went to the bathroom door. She could hear Ellen splashing in the tub. Linda opened the door. "Ellen," she said, "my shoestring is in a knot."

"Well, I can't help you now," said Ellen. "Wait until I finish my bath."

Linda closed the door. She stood in the middle of the room, looking up at her bunk. She wanted to get up there with Santhamum Rose and Whitey. She felt lonely. She didn't want to wait until Ellen had finished her bath. And where was Star? Why had she gone away and left her all alone?

Linda decided to get up in her bunk with Santhamum Rose and Whitey even though she still had one shoe on. She started to climb the ladder, first her soft right foot and then her hard left shoe—pat thump, pat thump, pat thump, until she reached the upper bunk. She had just settled herself under her covers when Star returned.

Star looked around the room. "Linda," she called, "where are you?"

"I'm up here," Linda replied. "Where did you go?"

"I went downstairs to get my doll."

Star got into her bunk and in a few minutes her mother came into the room to put out the light. "Linda," she said, "are you all right up there?"

For a second Linda thought of her shoe, but she decided not to mention it. If she did she would have to go down the ladder again. She hoped Ellen would forget all about it, too.

"I'm all right," said Linda.

"Well, now, go to sleep," said Mother. "Good night."

"Good night," the two little girls called back as the door closed.

Ellen did forget about Linda's shoe. She was busy thinking about the hot-water bottle that was hanging on a hook near the tub. It was pale blue and very pretty. The one at

Ellen's house was just rust color. She wished she could have the hot-water bottle to keep her feet warm. Just as Ellen came out of the bathroom, Betsy's mother came in to say good night. Betsy was sitting up in bed, reading a book.

"When you finish that chapter, Betsy, put the light out," said her mother.

"All right, Mother," replied Betsy.

"I wish I could have that lovely hot-water bottle for my feet," said Ellen.

"It isn't very cold tonight," said Betsy's mother.

"But my feet are always cold," said Ellen. "Even in the summertime."

"Well, of course you can have the hot-water bottle," said Mother. "I'll fill it for you."

"Oh, thank you, but I can fill it," said Ellen.

"Very well," said Mother. "Good night then."

Ellen returned to the bathroom and Betsy's mother closed the bedroom door. Ellen took the hot-water bottle off the hook and turned on the hot water. It wasn't so hot now that two baths had been run off, but it was very warm. Ellen decided that if she filled the bottle very full it would stay warm for a long time.

She hung over the side of the tub and held the rubber bottle under the faucet. She watched it grow fatter and fatter until it could hold no more. Then she turned the water off and put the stopper in the bottle. Before she carried it into the bedroom she dried it off with a towel. It felt heavy and warm as she carried it against her chest. She put it in her bed between the sheets and climbed in. With her feet she pushed the bottle down, down, down, until her legs were stretched out straight under the covers.

"I've finished my chapter," said Betsy. "Are you ready to have the light out?"

"Yes," replied Ellen. "My, but this bottle feels nice."

Betsy got up and opened the window. Then she got back into bed and switched out the light. The two girls lay in their beds looking up at the ceiling. A street lamp cast shadows of the bare branches of the trees on the ceiling. A stiff breeze blowing through the branches made an ever-changing pattern. Every once in a while Betsy would whisper, "Ellen, are you asleep?"

"Not yet," Ellen would reply. Then they would talk a little while, of school, of Mr. Kilpatrick's birthday party, and of what they wanted to do when they were grown up. Ellen said that she wanted to be an artist and make pictures for magazine covers. Betsy said she wanted to write books.

"And maybe I can make the pictures in your books," said Ellen.

"Oh, yes," said Betsy. "You can make all of the pictures in my books."

"I guess we better go to sleep," said Ellen.

"Yes," said Betsy. And they began again to

watch the shadows on the ceiling. Soon they were asleep.

Ellen began to dream. She dreamed that she was wading in a stream. The water felt warm as it lapped around her ankles and she could hear it gurgling. Suddenly she awoke with a start. Her feet felt wet. That was very strange, thought Ellen. She was lying in bed. How could she have wet feet? And then, all of a sudden, Ellen realized what was the matter. It was the hot-water bottle! Something had happened to the hot-water bottle!

Ellen threw back the covers and felt for the bottle. It was no longer fat and round. It was as flat as a flounder and the foot of the bed was soaking wet. Ellen picked up the limp bottle and placed it on the floor under the bed. She was pulling the covers off the bed when Betsy woke up.

"What's the matter?" said Betsy, sitting up in bed.

"Oh, Betsy," said Ellen, "something terrible happened! The hot-water bottle! It must have burst or something. All the water came out and my bed is soaking wet. What shall I do?"

Betsy jumped up and began to help Ellen take the bed covers off of the bed. The moon was shining in the sky outside the window. It was so bright that it made the street lamp look dim. The whole room was flooded with moonlight. It was so bright that Betsy did not bother to put on the light.

"What shall we do with the bed covers?" asked Ellen.

"I don't know," said Betsy. "They're so big."

"The blankets aren't wet," said Ellen. "Just the sheets and the mattress." The blankets they threw across the footboard.

"Let's put the sheets in the bathroom," said Betsy.

"Yes, that's a good idea," said Ellen.

They each carried a sheet into the bathroom. Ellen spread her sheet over the edge of the bathtub. Betsy did not know what to do with the sheet that she was holding. She looked around the bathroom and finally decided to try to hang it over the edge of the door. She carried a stool from the bedroom, climbed up, and flung the sheet over the corner of the door. "I guess it will stay there," she said as she climbed down. She put the stool back where it belonged and Ellen came into the bedroom, leaving the bathroom door ajar.

"You'll have to get in bed with me," said Betsy.

Betsy and Ellen got into bed and snuggled down under the warm covers. They were both very cold now. Soon they were both asleep again. They had been asleep about an hour when suddenly a piercing scream woke them both up.

Betsy sat up with a start. Rushing through the room in the moonlight, came what appeared to be a small white ghost. Ellen woke up. She had no idea where she was. She saw something white rushing around the room and to Ellen it seemed to fill the whole room. She was so frightened that she rolled over in the wrong direction and fell right out of bed.

Betsy sat as though frozen, her eyes as big as saucers and her heart beating like a hammer against her ribs. She couldn't move. She just sat and watched the creature as it leaped up and down. Then suddenly it fell to the floor, kicking and screaming.

Betsy was wide-awake now, and she knew that the white creature was Linda. It was

Linda lying on the floor, tangled up in a sheet. Betsy jumped out of bed. "Be quiet, Linda," she said, as she began to pull at the sheet. "Be quiet. You're all right. I'll get you out of this."

Ellen was under the bed. She looked out from between the two front legs. "What's the matter with her?" she said.

Linda sat up. She was crying very hard. "I was lonely!" she sobbed. "I came to find Ellen and something fell all over me in the bathroom. Something fell all over me," she wailed.

At this moment the door opened and Betsy's mother came in, in her dressing gown. "Whatever is the matter?" she said, switching on the light.

"It's Linda," said Betsy. "A sheet fell on her and she got awfully scared."

"But where was the sheet?" asked Mother.

"I hung it on the bathroom door to dry," said Betsy.

"To dry?" said her mother.

"Yes, it got wet when the hot-water bottle burst or something," said Betsy. "But we took all of the covers off and it's getting dry." Betsy felt the wet place on the bed.

"I'm sorry it bursted or something," said Ellen. "Maybe it didn't burst. Maybe it was just the stopper that came out."

"Maybe," said Betsy's mother, but she seemed to be thinking of something else. She was looking at Linda, who was now on her feet, rubbing the tears out of her eyes. Peeping out from under the hem of her nightgown were five tiny pink toes and the shiny brown toe of one of her new Oxfords.

"Linda," said Betsy's mother, "what are you doing with one shoe on?"

"I couldn't get it off," replied Linda. "It has a knot in it. I came to get Ellen to take it off."

"Come, sit on this chair and I'll take it off," said Betsy's mother. In a few minutes the shoe was off. "Now," said Mother, "I think it will be better if we put the two little girls in the same bed. Ellen, you go sleep in the upper bunk. That will give you and Betsy both more room."

Betsy went back to her bed, and Ellen and Linda went into Star's room. Star was still sound asleep when Linda got into the lower bunk and lay down beside her. Ellen climbed up the ladder into the upper bunk. Soon all was quiet again.

Ellen was just dozing off when Linda whispered from the lower bunk in a very loud whisper, "Ellen, will you hand me Santhamum Rose and Whitey?"

"No," said Ellen. "Go to sleep."

"You won't lie on them, will you?" said Linda.

"No," replied Ellen. "Go to sleep."

"They don't like to be laid on," said Linda.

"Go to sleep," said Ellen.

So Linda went to sleep and it was quiet the rest of the night.

CHAPTER 4
Easter Eggs

It was the Easter holidays and school was to be closed for a week. One afternoon Billy telephoned to Betsy. "Can you come over?" Billy asked when Betsy answered the telephone. "My mother says we can dye some eggs."

"I'd love to," said Betsy. "I have some wonderful decalcomanias that we can put on the eggs. Wait until I ask my mother if I can come over." Betsy ran upstairs to her

51

mother, who was hanging fresh curtains in Betsy's room. "Mother," said Betsy, "may I go over to Billy's house? He's dyeing Easter eggs."

"Of course," said Mother.

"And may I take some eggs to dye?" asked Betsy.

"Yes, you may take six," her mother answered.

"Oh, thank you," Betsy called back as she ran downstairs to the telephone. She picked up the telephone. "I'll be right over," she said.

"Swell!" said Billy, and he hung up.

Betsy went into the kitchen. She found an empty egg box on the shelf. She opened the refrigerator door and took out six eggs. She placed them in the box very carefully. When she arrived at Billy's house she said, "Mother gave me six eggs to dye."

"I have six too," said Billy. "Did you bring the decals you said you had?"

"Oh, I forgot them," said Betsy. "I'll go home and get them."

"Okay," said Billy. "While you're gone I'll boil the eggs. My mother has gone out."

Betsy set off for home. She ran most of the way.

Billy put some water into the small pan that his mother had given him to boil the eggs. Then he put his six eggs into the pan. It was much too full, so he took two of the eggs out and laid them on the table. Soon the eggs were boiling. "Ten minutes after they begin to boil," his mother had said. Billy set the timer on the front of the stove. He sat down on a kitchen stool and listened to it as it ticked away the minutes. Just as the bell on the timer rang, Betsy arrived with her decalcomanias.

"Let's see 'em," said Billy, as he took the eggs out of the pan and placed them on the table to cool.

Betsy spread the sheet of paper on the table. It was covered with gay pictures. There were bright-colored stripes, some in straight lines and some in circles. There were polka dots and stars and a lot of pictures.

"They're great!" said Billy. Then he pointed to some pictures of cats and dogs and said, "I'm going to use some of these for my eggs."

"But look at this one," said Betsy. "This is my favorite."

"Oh," said Billy, "it's a clown's face. It's good."

"I think it looks just like Humpty Dumpty," said Betsy.

"It is," cried Billy. "It is Humpty Dumpty. Is there another one like it? I would like to have a Humpty Dumpty egg."

The children bent their heads together and looked all over the sheet of decalcomanias for another Humpty Dumpty. They spent a long time examining the pictures and talking about them. At last Betsy said, "It's the only one. But you can have it, Billy."

"Oh, that's swell, Betsy," said Billy.

Betsy cut out the picture of Humpty Dumpty and handed it to Billy. "Thanks a lot, Betsy," he said. "I'm going to put that on my biggest egg."

"May I boil my eggs now?" Betsy asked.

"Sure," said Billy. "Here's the pan. You boil 'em ten minutes."

Betsy filled the pan with water. Then she asked, "Haven't you a bigger pan than this one? It won't hold all of my eggs."

"No, it won't," said Billy. "It only held four of mine." He opened a closet and pulled out a larger pan. "How about this?"

"Oh, that's all right," said Betsy, taking the pan from Billy.

"That's such a big pan, maybe you can do the rest of mine with yours," said Billy.

"Yes, there's plenty of room," replied Betsy, as she placed the last of her six eggs in the pan.

Billy pushed his largest egg to one side. "This is the one I'm going to use for Humpty Dumpty," he said.

"Which of yours aren't cooked?" said Betsy.

Billy looked at his eggs. Then he pointed to two of them. "Those two." Then he looked again. "No," he said, "one of those is cooked. It's these two that aren't."

Betsy picked them up one at a time. The second one felt a little warm, but Betsy thought nothing of that.

"After the water begins to boil, you set the timer for ten minutes," said Billy.

Betsy thought it took the water a very long time to boil, but after a while she heard it bubbling. Then she set the timer for ten minutes. Billy was busy transferring his picture of Humpty Dumpty to the smooth surface of his biggest egg. He worked very carefully, because he wanted it to be perfect. Betsy busied herself with selecting the six decalcomanias that she intended using on her eggs.

She cut them out of the sheet and laid them aside. When the bell on the timer rang, Betsy turned off the heat and placed the pan of eggs in the sink. She turned on the cold water to cool them.

"May I do one of your eggs while I'm waiting for mine to get cold?" she asked. "Then you can do one of mine."

"Okay," said Billy.

Billy was removing his decalcomania very carefully, lifting it by one corner. "Oh, Betsy," he said, "this is keen! It's coming off perfectly."

Betsy picked up one of Billy's eggs from the table and set to work decorating it with the face of a cat. In a moment Billy held up Humpty Dumpty. "Look, Betsy," he said.

"That's perfect," said Betsy.

"I'm going to make a paper collar for him," said Billy.

"Oh, that's a good idea," said Betsy.

Billy set to work with a paper cup and scissors and soon he had made a collar for Humpty Dumpty. He was delighted with the result. By this time Betsy had finished the cat. It was a great success too.

When Billy's mother returned, all the eggs were decorated. They looked very gay.

"What beautiful Easter eggs!" said Mrs. Porter.

"Look at Humpty Dumpty," said Billy. "It's the best of all."

"Oh, he's very handsome," said Mrs. Porter.

"It was the only one on the whole sheet of decals," said Billy, "and Betsy gave it to me."

"That was very generous of Betsy," said Mrs. Porter.

Betsy put her eggs back in the egg box and rolled up the remains of her decalcomanias. "I have to go now," she said. "I've had a very nice time."

"Thanks again for Humpty Dumpty," said Billy. "I'm going to keep him a long time before I eat him."

"You sound like a cannibal," laughed Betsy, "when you say you're going to eat him."

"Maybe I'll never eat him," said Billy. "Maybe I'll just keep him."

"But eggs get bad if you keep them too long," said Betsy.

"Oh, not if they're hard-boiled," said Billy.

"Well, if they're hard-boiled you can keep them longer," said Betsy, "but you can't keep them too long. They get bad."

"Not Humpty Dumpty," said Billy. "He's what you call a good egg."

The children laughed and Billy began to sing over and over, "Humpty Dumpty, he's a good egg! Humpty Dumpty, he's a good egg." As Betsy walked down the street she could still hear Billy shouting, "Humpty Dumpty, he's a good egg!"

Billy went back to the kitchen. He took a soup dish and filled it with some green tissue paper. Then he put his eggs in the dish. He placed Humpty Dumpty in the center. It made such a gay nest that Billy's mother told him to put it on the dining-room table for a centerpiece.

On Easter Sunday there was an Easter basket for Billy, filled with chocolate eggs. In the afternoon his grandmother arrived with another Easter basket of chocolate eggs.

During the following week Billy seemed to be eating Easter eggs every time his mother looked at him. Soon all the eggs were gone. Even the colored ones from the center of the table disappeared—all but Humpty Dumpty. Finally he sat alone in the nest of green tissue paper.

On Saturday Mrs. Porter moved it to the

shelf in the kitchen. There sat Humpty Dumpty in his collar, which was no longer white. He sat there for several weeks. Then one afternoon Billy's father noticed Humpty Dumpty. "This egg has been here for ages," he said. "I don't believe Billy wants it any longer." Just as his father picked up Humpty Dumpty, Billy came into the kitchen. When he saw his father with Humpty Dumpty he cried out, "Daddy! Don't take Humpty Dumpty! I want to keep him."

"Oh," said his father, "I thought you didn't want it. I'm tired of seeing it around."

"Sure I want it," said Billy. "I'll take it to school. I'll keep it in my desk."

"I hope it's all right," said Mr. Porter.

Billy took it in his hand and looked at it carefully. "It's okay," he said. "Humpty Dumpty's still a good egg."

The next morning Billy took his egg to school with him. He put it in his pocket very carefully, so that he would not muss Humpty Dumpty's collar. On his way to school he met Betsy. "I've got Humpty Dumpty with me," he said.

"You mean you still have that old egg left from Easter?" said Betsy.

"Humpty Dumpty's a good egg," said Billy.

"Where is it?" Betsy asked.

"In my pocket," replied Billy.

"Well, you can't eat it," said Betsy. "It's been around too long."

Billy took the egg out of his pocket. "Oh, I don't know," he said. "Maybe I'll eat it and maybe I won't." He tapped the egg gently against his front teeth.

They had reached the corner where Mr. Kilpatrick took the children across the wide avenue. He had just crossed the avenue with a group of kindergarten children. Betsy and Billy waited for him to return.

"I'll bet Mr. Kilpatrick would like to have Humpty Dumpty," said Billy. "I'll bet he would like him."

"Why don't you give it to him?" said Betsy.

"Maybe I will," said Billy.

When Mr. Kilpatrick returned he said, "Hello, Billy!" Then, looking at Betsy, he said, "How are you this morning, Red Ribbons?"

"Fine, thanks," replied Betsy.

"Would you like to have Humpty Dumpty, Mr. Kilpatrick?" asked Billy, holding up his egg.

"Say now, that's a mighty pretty egg," said Mr. Kilpatrick, taking it in his hand.

"You can have it, Mr. Kilpatrick," said Billy.

"Thank you very much, Billy," said Mr. Kilpatrick, "but I don't care for eggs." He handed the egg back.

"Okay," said Billy, "but it's a very good egg."

"Don't doubt it," replied Mr. Kilpatrick, "if you like eggs."

When Billy reached school, he showed Humpty Dumpty to all of the boys and girls. "Is it an Easter egg?" asked Ellen.

"Sure," said Billy.

"But Easter was a long time ago," said Kenny.

"I kept it," said Billy.

"It looks awful old," said Christopher.

"It's a good egg," said Billy. "It's just a little dusty."

"I don't think it's any good," said Betsy.

"Sure it's good," said Billy. "It's hard-boiled."

When the bell rang for school to begin, Miss Ross said, "Now, Billy, put the egg out of sight. We all have work to do."

Billy put the egg in his pocket and opened his book for the reading lesson. Miss Ross

asked the poor readers to come up to the front of the room. "The rest of the class may read quietly," said Miss Ross. Billy was a good reader and he liked to read. He sat at his desk in the back of the room with his book open in front of him.

In a few minutes his hand went into his pocket. It touched Humpty Dumpty. He lifted it out and held it in his hand. He stopped reading and looked at it. He guessed that he would eat it at recess. "Might as well take the shell off," he said to himself.

Billy lifted the egg to the top of his desk and tapped it just once. The shell broke, and to Billy's surprise water seemed to be running over his desk. He looked at it and saw that there was something yellow, too.

Without thinking, Billy put his arm over the mess to try to mop it up with the sleeve of his sweater. There was a very bad odor.

"Phew!" cried Christopher, who sat behind Billy. "What stinks?"

"Christopher!" said Miss Ross. "What kind of language is that!"

"What smells?" said Christopher.

"Smells like rotten eggs," cried Kenny.

Now all of the children were saying, "Phew!"

Miss Ross got up. She walked to the back of the room. "What is that terrible odor?" she said. Billy had both arms over his desk and his face was bright red. "Billy," said Miss Ross, "what on earth have you been doing?"

"It's my egg," said Billy. "I guess it was never cooked."

When Miss Ross saw the sleeves of Billy's sweater, she said, "Billy, you will have to go home at once and change your sweater. We cannot have you in school in that condition."

Billy got up. "I can take it off," he said. "I have a shirt under it."

"But we can't have anything that smells like that sweater in the school," said Miss Ross.

"I'm sorry, Miss Ross," said Billy.

"I hope so," said Miss Ross. "Now you see what happens when you are disobedient. I told you not to play with that egg. I shall have to mark you zero for everything you miss while you go home. And before you go, take a cloth and wash the top of your desk."

Miss Ross opened the windows as wide as she could while Billy washed the top of his desk. Then he departed. Near the gate of the schoolyard, Billy found a long stick that some child had thrown away. He picked it up.

About ten o'clock, Billy's mother went to the mailbox to mail a letter. She looked up the street and saw Billy coming. She wondered why he was coming home at this time in the morning and she wondered why he was carrying a pole over his shoulder with his sweater hanging from the end like a flag.

CHAPTER 5
Pansies Are Notions

On her way to school Betsy had to pass by a group of stores. There was Roger's grocery store, Weaver's drugstore, Mike's shoe-repair shop, the Don't Forget card shop and Hardy's flower shop.

Between the card shop and the flower shop there had been an empty store for quite a long time. The window was dirty, the paint on the door had peeled off, and the spiders had hung their cobwebs both inside and out. A *For Rent* sign was painted on the center of the window.

FOR RENT

FIRST NATIONAL BANK
NORTH STREET BRANCH OFFICE.

One of the games that Betsy played with Ellen or with Billy when they walked home from school was "Guess What I'm Going to Buy!" As the children came to each store, they would look in the window and one would say to the other, "Guess what I'm going to buy in this store." When they looked in the window of the card shop, the question was "Guess what kind of a card I'm going to buy in this store." And in front of the flower shop it was "Guess what kind of a flower I'm going to buy in this store." Of course they never bought anything, but only made believe.

When they reached the empty store they would just pass quickly by, but one day when Betsy and Billy were playing the game Billy stopped and said, "Guess what I'm going to buy in this store."

"Nothing!" Betsy cried out.

"Wrong!" shouted Billy.

"There's nothing to buy," said Betsy.

"There is! There is!" cried Billy. "Guess what I'm going to buy!"

"I give up," said Betsy.

"A cobweb!" Billy shouted.

The children laughed, and after that they always called the shop the Cobweb store.

One day when Betsy was walking home from school she was surprised to see that the *For Rent* sign was off the Cobweb shop and the windows had been cleaned. The next day a painter was busy painting the door and all the woodwork. All the cobwebs were gone.

"Somebody is moving into the Cobweb store," said Betsy to Billy.

"I hope it's a candy store," said Billy.

Several days later, when Betsy and Ellen were walking home from school, they found that a sign had been placed above the window of the shop. It said *Mrs. McVittie's— Notions.*

"Mrs. McVittie's—Notions," Betsy read aloud. Then she said, "What are notions?"

"Notions?" said Ellen. "Why, you know. Mummy says my brother Jack gets crazy notions. Like when he wanted to jump off the kitchen roof with an umbrella because he said he wanted to be a paratrooper."

"But that isn't anything you can sell," said Betsy.

"Well, that's what a notion is, anyway," said Ellen. "It's something you think of. Mummy is always saying, 'People have funny notions.' "

"Like funny thoughts?" said Betsy.

"That's right," replied Ellen.

For several days when Betsy passed the shop she always looked in the window to see if there was anything to look at, but it was always empty. She could hardly wait to see what Mrs. McVittie's notions would be. At last the day came when Betsy looked in the window and found something in it. She was surprised to find some bright-colored aprons draped across the back of the window. In the center were several pincushions. On one side there were boxes of children's socks and on the other there were boys' suspenders. In the very front of the window Betsy found a row of little boxes. She looked them over very carefully, trying to find something that would show the reason why Mrs. McVittie's sign said *Notions*.

Some of the boxes contained earrings with brightly colored stones. Others held pins that sparkled. Then Betsy's eye fell upon one box that was right at the end of the row. It held a pin that Betsy thought was the most beautiful of all. It was made to look exactly like a purple pansy and it had a sparkling stone in the center that looked like a diamond.

The pin was fastened to a white card and on the card Betsy read the words *Pansies for Thoughts*.

Betsy was delighted. Here was a notion! She didn't know about all of the other things, but the pansy was certainly a notion, because it said, right on the card, that it was for thoughts and Ellen had said that notions were thoughts. Only this pansy pin was not a funny notion or a crazy notion. It was a beautiful notion. Betsy stood so long before the window that she was almost late for school. She had to run all the way, but she was thinking about the pansy pin, for it had given her an idea.

Next Sunday was Mother's Day and Betsy had been trying to think of a present for Mother. Now she knew what she wanted to give her. Nothing could be as nice, thought Betsy, as the pansy pin.

When Betsy reached school she said to Ellen, "Did you see the notion in Mrs. McVittie's window?"

"No," said Ellen. "I came to school on the bus."

"Oh, it's beautiful," said Betsy. "It's a pansy pin."

"How can a pansy pin be a notion?" asked Ellen.

"But it says right on the card—*Pansies for Thoughts,*" said Betsy.

After school Betsy and Ellen walked home together. When they reached Mrs. McVittie's shop they stood for a long time looking in the window. Ellen agreed with Betsy that the pansy pin was beautiful.

"I want to buy it for my mother for Mother's Day," said Betsy.

"Oh, that would be nice," said Ellen. "Do you have any money?"

"I have some in my little old bank," said Betsy. "I'm going in and ask how much it is."

The two children went into the store. There was a long counter filled with boxes and behind the counter was the tallest woman Betsy had ever seen. She was busy placing the boxes on the shelves that filled the wall behind the counter. Betsy guessed that this was Mrs. McVittie.

Betsy stepped up to the counter and watched Mrs. McVittie as she stretched out her long arm and placed a box on the very top shelf. When she turned around she saw Betsy and said, "Did you wish to buy something?"

"I just wanted to know how much the pansy notion is?" said Betsy.

"The what?" asked Mrs. McVittie.

"The pansy pin in the window," said Betsy.

"Oh," said Mrs. MicVittie. "I'll have to see."

Mrs. McVittie came out from behind the counter, and Betsy followed her to the little door that opened into the window. Mrs. McVittie opened the door, and with her long arm she reached farther and farther into the window until she picked up the box with the pansy pin. She held it out to Betsy and said, "It's one dollar and ninety-five cents."

"Oh," said Betsy. "Well, I haven't any money with me today, but if I have enough in my bank I should like to buy it for my mother, for Mother's Day."

Mrs. McVittie smiled. "Now that's a nice notion," said Mrs. McVittie.

Betsy's face lighted up and she said, "Oh, I think it's much better than nice. I think it's a beautiful one."

Mrs. McVittie looked a little surprised and said, "Would you like me to keep this for you until you see if you have enough money? It's the only one I have."

"Oh, yes! Please do," said Betsy.

Betsy and Ellen said good-by as they went out of the store. "I do hope I have enough money," said Betsy, when they were on the sidewalk. When she got home she went right to her room. She took the key to her bank out of a little jewelry box that she kept on the table beside her bed. Then she took her bank from the top of her bookshelves and opened it. She poured out the money on her bed. It looked like a lot, but Betsy noticed that there were a good many pennies.

Betsy sat down on the bed and counted her money. It came to one dollar and seven cents. Betsy thought that was pretty far away from one dollar and ninety-five cents. "Oh, dear!" she said. "I'll never be able to save up enough by next Friday." It was already Tuesday.

Betsy decided that she would try to earn the money. How much did she need? She opened her desk and took out a pencil and paper. She wrote down $1.95 and put $1.07 under it. She knew that she had to take away $1.07 from $1.95 and that the answer would be the amount of money she would have to earn. Soon she had the answer. It was eighty-eight cents that she needed.

Eighty-eight cents! thought Betsy. What could she do to earn eighty-eight cents?

One day she had earned fifty cents when she sat with Mrs. White's baby while Mrs. White did some shopping. Mrs. White lived around the corner from Betsy's house. Maybe Mrs. White would like her to sit with the baby again.

Betsy put her money back in her bank and ran off to see Mrs. White. She rang the doorbell and Mrs. White opened the door. "Hello, Betsy," she said.

"Hello, Mrs. White," said Betsy. "I thought maybe you might like me to sit with the baby while you do some shopping."

"Well, not today, Betsy, but I'd like you to come next Wednesday," said Mrs. White.

"Oh, that would be too late," said Betsy. "Couldn't you please go shopping this week?"

"I suppose I could go on Saturday," said Mrs. White.

"Oh, not Saturday," said Betsy. "I have to get it on Friday."

"What do you have to get, Betsy?" asked Mrs. White.

"The notion for Mother's Day," replied Betsy. "Mrs. McVittie is keeping it for me until Friday."

"Now I see," said Mrs. White. "You want to earn some money to buy your mother a present."

"That's it," said Betsy.

"Very well," said Mrs. White. "I'll do my shopping tomorrow. Come tomorrow after school."

The next day Betsy hurried home from school and ran around the corner to Mrs. White's house. When she arrived the baby was asleep, and Mrs. White went off to do her shopping. When she returned Betsy said, "The baby is still asleep. It was very easy to take care of her."

"Yes," said Mrs. White, "but I could not have gone away and left her alone."

"Well, thank you very much," said Betsy when Mrs. White gave her fifty cents. "Any time at all I'll be glad to come over."

"Thank you, Betsy," said Mrs. White.

Betsy ran home with her fifty cents. She went up to her room and opened her bank. She counted her money again. Now she had $1.57. Again she put the figures down on a piece of paper. She still needed thirty-eight cents before she could buy the present for Mother. She wished that her father were home. He would lend me thirty-eight cents, thought Betsy. But Father was away and would not be back until Saturday night.

Friday came at last and Betsy had only one dollar and fifty-seven cents in her pocketbook. On her way home from school she went into Mrs. McVittie's shop. Some girls from the high school were standing at the counter. As Betsy stepped up to the counter, she heard Mrs. McVittie say, "Here's the little girl now that I was saving it for."

Betsy saw that one of the girls was holding the pansy pin in her hand.

She looked at Betsy and said, "Are you going to buy this? If you're not going to buy it, I want it for my mother for Mother's Day."

"I can't buy it," said Betsy. "I don't have enough money."

"Oh, well, then I'll take it," said the girl.

Betsy turned and ran out of the shop. There was such a big lump in her throat that she could hardly swallow. Then the tears came and she began to cry. The lovely pansy pin was gone—gone to someone else's mother. It was such a lovely notion, thought Betsy to herself. A pansy for thoughts.

Betsy didn't want anyone to see her crying,

so she stood by the side of the flower shop with her face turned away from the sidewalk where the children from school were passing. She could hear them chattering.

Suddenly Betsy's pocketbook slipped out of her hand. She stooped down to pick it up and, as she did, she looked right into a box of pansy plants. Then she saw that there was a whole row of boxes of pansy plants at her feet. They were beautiful pansies, dark purple and pale blue, big yellow ones with dark centers and white ones with violet edges. Betsy looked down at them and they seemed to look up at her like little faces.

Then Betsy had an idea. Why, here were a lot of pansies for thoughts. Not the lovely notion that the pansy pin was, but if she could buy Mother a pansy plant she was sure that Mother would like it. As she went into the flower shop, Betsy hoped she had enough money to buy a plant.

A man came out from the back of the shop and said, "Did you want something?"

"How much are the pansy plants?" asked Betsy.

"Seventy-five cents a box," replied the man.

"For a whole box?" said Betsy.

"Yes," replied the man. "They are very fine plants. Six plants in a box."

Betsy opened her pocketbook and counted out seventy-five cents. She felt very rich when she saw how much change she had left.

"I'll put a paper around the box," said the man. "It will be easier to carry."

Betsy carried her parcel very carefully. She did not want to break off any of the flowers. She was glad that her mother had gone to help Mrs. Porter make some curtains. She would be able to hide the box of pansies until Sunday. She put the box of pansies in the garage, back behind the wheelbarrow.

On Saturday Betsy watered the pansies and picked off a few of the flowers that had faded. More buds had opened, and the box of pansies looked even more beautiful than it had when Betsy bought it.

Before breakfast on Sunday morning Betsy carried the box of pansies into the house. Mother was in the kitchen making pancakes for breakfast.

"Mother," said Betsy, "this is your present for Mother's Day."

Mother turned and looked at Betsy. "Why, Betsy darling!" she cried. "How lovely!"

"Well, there was something nicer that I wanted to get for you. It was a lovely notion, Mother. It was a pansy pin."

"Oh, but these are much nicer," said Mother, "because these I shall plant in the garden and there will be more and more all through the summer. We'll pick them and they will make the house beautiful."

"I'm glad you like them, Mother," said Betsy. "Did you know that pansies are for notions?"

"You mean pansies are for thoughts, dear," said Mother.

"But the pansy pin at Mrs. McVittie's was a notion, Mother. Because the sign on Mrs. McVittie's store says *Mrs. McVittie's—Notions*. I wonder why it doesn't say *Mrs. McVittie's—Thoughts*."

Mother laughed. "Oh, Betsy darling," she said, "there are other notions besides thoughts. A notion store is a store that sells all kinds of things. Pins and needles and thread and elastic and hooks and eyes. All kinds of things for sewing—they're all notions."

"Well!" said Betsy. "I'll have to tell Ellen that she doesn't know everything about notions."

CHAPTER 6

The Circus Comes to Town

One morning circus signs were on all of the billboards—big pictures of clowns, lion tamers, elephants, beautiful ladies riding bareback horses, men and women flying through the air from one trapeze to another. There were seals balancing big balls on their noses and dancing poodle dogs.

Betsy and her friends were so excited they could hardly keep their minds on their lessons. More than once Miss Ross had to speak to Billy Porter for not paying attention during the arithmetic lesson and even Ellen, who was always as good as gold, drew a clown on her spelling paper.

"Really," said Miss Ross, "I don't know what is the matter with you children this morning."

"It's the circus," said Billy. "The circus is coming. Boy! I can't wait."

"Did you see the big signs, Miss Ross?" said Betsy. "It looks wonderful."

"It's coming next week," said Kenny. "My father's going to take me."

This remark started a whole chorus from the other children. "Oh, my father's going to take me, too." "My mother said she would take me."

"Well," said Miss Ross, "as long as you are all so much interested in the circus this morning, suppose we write stories about the circus."

"Swell," said Billy, who loved to write stories.

The children looked pleased as Miss Ross handed out sheets of yellow paper.

"What shall we write about the circus?" Kenny asked.

"Oh, there are many things to write about,"

said Miss Ross. "You can write about the first time you ever went to the circus."

Mary Lou raised her hand. "Yes, Mary Lou," said Miss Ross.

"I've never been to the circus," said Mary Lou.

"Write about the circus parade that we all saw last year," said Miss Ross.

"I didn't see the circus parade," said Mary Lou. "I had the mumps."

"Then just write about what you saw on the big signs this morning," said Miss Ross.

"I didn't see the signs," said Mary Lou.

"Mary Lou," said Miss Ross, "would you like to go to the circus?"

"Oh, yes," said Mary Lou.

"Well, just write why you would like to go," said Miss Ross.

Mary Lou sat down and this is what she wrote: "I would like to go to the cercus to see the ellapants. The ellapants have long drunks and they eat P nuts. I saw the ellapants in the soo."

Miss Ross said she would like some of the children to read their stories. Billy's hand went into the air right away. "I see Billy wants to read his," she said.

Billy stood up. This is what he read: "The last time I went to the circus an elephant lifted me up in his trunk and I rode all around on top of the elephant."

"Oh!" cried the children.

"I don't believe it," said Kenny.

"Billy," said Miss Ross, "this is supposed to be a true story, not a make-believe one."

"Oh!" said Billy. "Well, it could be true."

"That doesn't make any difference," said Miss Ross. "You must write about something that happened to you. You see, we all knew that wasn't true, Billy."

"How did you know?" said Billy.

Just then the bell rang for lunch, so it was Kenny who answered Billy's question as they walked out of the room. "Because," said Kenny, "things like that don't happen when you go to the circus."

The circus was to arrive the following Sunday, when Billy's grandfather was visiting the Porters. In the afternoon Grandfather said, "Billy, suppose we get Betsy and drive over to the circus grounds and see what is going on."

"Oh, swell!" said Billy, and he rushed to the telephone and called Betsy.

Betsy was delighted to go. She was waiting by the front gate when they arrived. "I'm so excited," she said. "I never saw a circus arrive."

"Well, I'm sure it won't be as exciting for me as it was when I was a boy," said Grandfather. "The circus used to come on the railroad then. It all came in big railroad cars—all painted up. It made a mighty gay train. I can remember the thrill of seeing it roll into town. Now it's all done with trucks and trailers." Grandfather chuckled. "I used to carry buckets of water for the elephants," he said. "My, how those elephants could drink! I used to get a ticket to the circus for carrying the water."

"Could I carry water for the elephants?" said Billy.

"No, those days are over," said his grandfather. "Nobody gets near the elephants now but the people employed in the circus."

Soon they reached the circus grounds. Everything was in a hubbub. The big tent was already up, but little tents and booths were cropping up like so many little chicks around a big mother hen.

Heavy ropes had been put up to keep peo-

ple out of the grounds until all was ready.
The ropes were lined with people watching
the workmen as they ran back and forth. The
shouting and the hammering raised a terrible
din and through it all came the music of a
merry-go-round. The merry-go-round was outside of the ropes. It was already filled with
children.

"Can we go on the merry-go-round, Gramp?"
said Billy.

"Yes," said his grandfather. "If you can
find an animal without a rider. It looks filled
up to me."

"Oh, there'll be some getting off when it
stops," said Betsy.

Grandfather bought two tickets from the
man in the ticket booth near the merry-go-
round. He handed one to Billy and one to
Betsy. They thanked Grandfather and joined
the crowd of children who were waiting to
ride.

The merry-go-round was slowing down now.
It went slower and slower until finally it
stopped. Betsy was right. Most of the children got off, and the waiting crowd bumped
into them as they scrambled aboard. Each
one seemed to have picked out a favorite

steed so that there was a great deal of rushing and clambering before the new riders were in the saddle.

Billy had chosen a handsome black horse, but when he reached it he saw the rider had stayed on for another ride. He was a boy about Billy's age. He had curly black hair and dark brown eyes that seemed almost black. Billy climbed on the only thing that was left. It was right beside the black horse. He was disappointed because it was not on the outside of the merry-go-round, but he liked his mount even though it was only a white horse.

Betsy was riding a handsome zebra. In front of her was a little girl on a goat. She had a mop of black curls. Once she turned around and looked at Betsy. Betsy smiled and said, "Hello!"

"Hello!" replied the girl.

When the merry-go-round stopped, Billy and Betsy were sorry to get off. Billy ran to his grandfather and said, "Gramp, can't I ride again? I want to ride on the outside. I didn't get the horse I wanted 'cause some boy stayed on. Can I go again, Gramp?"

"Well, this is the last time," said his

grandfather, as he walked over to the ticket booth.

When the merry-go-round stopped, the children climbed aboard once more. Billy rushed around to the opposite side to find the black horse. To his sorrow, there sat the black-haired boy. He seemed to be glued to the

black horse. "Are you going to stay on that horse forever?" said Billy.

The boy opened his eyes in surprise and said, "Do you want to ride this horse?"

"Yes," said Billy. "He's just the kind of a horse I'd like to have."

"Okay," said the boy, and he climbed down.

"Oh, thanks," said Billy, his face all a big smile. "That's swell!"

"Oh, I can ride it all day," said the boy.

"What do you mean, you can ride it all day?" Billy asked.

"Oh, my uncle owns this merry-go-round," replied the boy.

Billy let out a long whistle. "Whee!" he said. "You sure are lucky."

When Betsy and Billy had finished their second ride, they walked away with Billy's grandfather. Not far from the merry-go-round a hot-dog stand had sprung up and the owner was already in business. Customers crowded around.

"Can I have a hot dog, Gramp?" said Billy.

"Now you can't have everything you see," said his grandfather. "There's a frozen custard stand over there. You can either have a hot dog or a frozen custard. Which do you want?"

"I want the hot dog," said Billy.

"What do you want, Betsy?" said his grandfather.

"The hot dog, please," said Betsy.

Just as Billy was about to take a bite out of his roll, he saw the boy who had given up the horse on the merry-go-round. He was with a little girl who looked just like him.

"Hi!" shouted Billy. The boy waved his hand. "He's a friend of mine," said Billy to Betsy. "His uncle owns the merry-go-round. He can ride on it all day if he wants to."

Betsy looked at the boy. Then she recognized the girl. "Oh!" she said. "That girl was on the goat in front of me."

The two curlyheads went up to the counter and soon each one had a roll. Billy's grandfather met an old friend of his and they began to talk about the circus when they were boys. Billy and Betsy walked over to the two children from the merry-go-round. "Did you get tired of riding?" said Billy.

"Got hungry," said the boy.

"I like that black horse," said Billy. "It's my favorite. I wish I could have a real live horse like that one."

"My mother's got a white horse," said the boy.

"Does she let you ride it?" asked Billy.

"Sure," said the boy.

"I wish they had elephants on the merry-go-round," said Billy. "They have every kind of animal except an elephant. Why don't you ask your uncle to put an elephant on?"

"I ride on real elephants," said the boy, taking a large bite of hot dog.

"You can't make me believe that," said Billy. "Where would you get an elephant to ride on?"

"My father has five elephants," said the boy.

"Your mother has a white horse, your father has five elephants," said Billy, laughing. "What else do you have? See if you can make me believe it."

"We've got six poodles and three seals," said the boy.

The girl pointed to a big circus poster pasted on the side of a truck that was standing nearby. It was a picture of a beautiful lady dancing on the back of a white horse. "That's my mother," she said.

Betsy and Billy regarded the picture in silence.

"Come here," said the boy, leading the way around to the other side of the truck. There was another picture. It showed a man wearing shiny boots, tight black trousers, a red coat with tails, and a high hat. Five elephants were standing up in front of him. "And that's my father," said the boy, waving the remains of his hot dog at the big poster.

Billy and Betsy were speechless. Finally Billy said, "What's your name?"

"Tony," said the boy.

"I'm Tina," said the girl. "We're twins."

"Where do you live?" asked Betsy.

"We live in the circus trailer," said Tony. "It's over the other side of the tent."

Billy gulped and his eyes almost popped out. "Do you live with all those animals?" he asked. "The elephants and everything?"

"Just with the poodles," said Tony. "The other animals are all outside."

Billy gasped. "Tony," he said, "could I come over and play at your house some day?"

"Sure," said Tony.

"Can I come too?" asked Betsy.

"Of course," said Tina.

Just then Billy's grandfather came up to the children. "Come along now," he said. "It's time we were getting home."

"Well, so long," said Billy. "I'll be seeing you."

"So long," said Tony.

"Good-by," said Betsy.

"Good-by," said Tina. "Don't forget to come and play."

"Forget!" exclaimed Billy. "How could I forget? Elephants and poodles and seals and everything!"

As Billy and Betsy walked away with Grandfather, Billy said, "Betcha I'll get a ride on one of those elephants and won't Miss Ross be surprised!"

"We don't know what their last name is," said Betsy. "We ought to know what their last name is. How'll we find them when we come over to play with them if we don't know what their last name is?"

"That's right," said Billy, and he turned and ran after the children. When he caught up to them he said, "What's your last name, Tony?"

"Pappagottapotchi," said Tony.

"Thanks," said Billy.

When he caught up with Betsy and his grandfather again, Betsy said, "Did you find out what their last name is?"

"It sounds like 'Papa's got something,' but I don't know what it is he's got," said Billy.

"But it doesn't matter. All we have to say is 'We want to see Tony and Tina. Their father's the elephant, seal, and poodle trainer.' "

"Billy," said Betsy, "do you think it's true?"

Billy looked surprised. "Sure it's true," he said. "Sure it is. And I bet you I'll ride on one of those elephants. And his uncle owns the merry-go-round! Boy! Oh, boy!"

CHAPTER 7
The Circus Parade

On Monday morning, when Betsy and Billy reached school, they could talk of nothing but their new friends at the circus. It was hard to get the children in their class to listen, because they were all so excited about the circus parade. The circus parade was to pass the school at ten o'clock and all the children in the school would see it. They were to stand on the sidewalk and watch the parade.

When the bell rang for school to begin, the boys and girls could not seem to quiet down. Many of them had been to the circus grounds on Sunday and they all wanted to talk about it.

"Now, boys and girls," said Miss Ross, as she passed out yellow paper. "We are going to have our arithmetic lesson."

"Oh!" several of the children groaned.

"We are going to have story examples," said Miss Ross. The children brightened. "You will write the answer on your paper," said Miss Ross. "Just the answer. Listen carefully. If there are eight clowns in the circus ring and three of the clowns ride away on bicycles, how many clowns are left?"

"Easy," said Kenny.

"Quiet, Kenny," said Miss Ross.

The children thought for a moment, and then every head bent over and a figure appeared on each paper. When the children looked up, Miss Ross said, "There are seven elephants in the ring." Billy raised his hand. "Yes, Billy?" said Miss Ross.

"There are only five," said Billy. "I know, because they belong to my friend Tony's father."

"Billy, that has nothing to do with our examples," said Miss Ross. "Now I'll repeat. There are seven elephants in the ring. Four are sitting up. How many elephants are standing?"

Every face was turned to Miss Ross. As each child thought of the answer a smile spread over his face. Then a second figure appeared on the yellow papers.

"Now listen again," said Miss Ross. Every eye was upon the teacher. "There are six horses in the ring. Two are ridden by bareback riders." Billy and Betsy both raised their hands. "Yes, Betsy?" said Miss Ross.

"My friend Tina's mother is a bareback rider," said Betsy.

"She's Tony's sister," Billy called out.

"Will you please stop interrupting?" said Miss Ross. "If there are six horses in the ring and two are ridden by bareback riders, how many horses are without riders?"

Again the children wrote the answer on their papers. Miss Ross continued with more examples until the children had a long list of figures on their papers. Then she asked Billy to collect the papers. At half past nine the bell rang. It meant that the children were to

march out and take their places on the sidewalk to see the circus parade. Their faces
were covered with smiles.

"The parade is coming!" said Kenny.

"I'll bet Tina will be in it," said Betsy to
Ellen.

"Who is Tina?" Ellen asked.

"Oh, she's my new friend," said Betsy, as
they formed in line. "Her mother owns a
beautiful white horse and she rides it in the
circus."

Billy pushed his way in behind Betsy. "Her
brother is Tony," he said. "And their father
has five elephants and they have trained poodle dogs and seals."

"Be quiet, boys and girls," said Miss Ross.

Kenny, who was behind Billy, whispered,
"I don't believe it."

"It's true," whispered Billy. "Ask Betsy."

"You and Betsy just made it up," Kenny
whispered back.

"Kenny!" said Miss Ross. "One more word
out of you or Billy, and you will both stay in
the room and miss the parade."

Kenny's and Billy's ears turned bright red.
Not another word was spoken until they
reached the sidewalk. Then Billy said to Betsy,

"I'll bet Tony and Tina will be riding on the elephants."

"Or maybe on horses," said Betsy.

"Go on! Quit kidding," said Kenny. "There's no such kid as Tony and there's no Tina."

"You just wait," said Billy. "You'll see."

"They'll be along soon," said Betsy.

Suddenly a wave of children's voices rose. "Here it comes!"

Very faintly in the distance music sounded. It was a band playing. A thrill went right down Betsy's backbone. She leaned against the rope that had been stretched from telegraph pole to telegraph pole and looked up the street. She could see the band marching forward, growing larger and larger. The music sounded louder and louder. Soon it was close enough for Betsy to see that a red police car was leading the whole parade. She wondered if it was Mr. Kilpatrick's car. Now it had reached the far end of the line of children. They were waving and shouting. "Hi, Mr. Kilpatrick!"

As the car rolled slowly past Betsy's class, the children waved and shouted, "Hi, Mr. Kilpatrick!" Mr. Kilpatrick waved back.

Now the band was very loud, for it was

passing Betsy. The big drum seemed to be right inside her head, it was so loud. Behind the band was a beautiful white horse and on the horse sat the bareback rider, smiling and waving to the children.

"There's Tony's mother!" cried Billy, and he waved his hand and jumped up and down.

"You're crazy, Billy," said Kenny. "That's a bareback rider. She isn't anybody's mother."

"She is so," said Betsy.

"I don't believe it," said Christopher.

Now the elephants were passing. On the back of the first elephant was a little house, and inside sat a man dressed in a purple and gold robe. On his head he wore a purple silk turban, wound around and around with pearls and sparkling stones.

"I'll bet that's Tony's father," cried Billy, waving his hand.

"I guess it is," said Betsy.

Billy cupped his hands around his mouth and shouted to the man on the elephant, "Where's Tony?" But the man made no reply. He just bowed and waved to the children.

"Aw, cut this stuff out," said Kenny. "Where are those kids, Tony and Tina? Show 'em to me."

"They'll be along pretty soon," said Betsy. "Just wait."

"I'm waiting," said Christopher. "Aren't you, Kenny?"

Kenny winked at Christopher and said, "You bet."

On the head of one of the elephants rode a clown. He waved a huge white hand at the children. Behind the elephants came a cage with two lions, then one filled with monkeys. The seals were splashing around in a tank of water on a big truck. The trucks and the cages rolled by, each one gayer than the last. Betsy and Billy watched for Tony and Tina, but they saw nothing of the black-haired twins.

The parade was almost over now. Betsy was looking down the street. She could already see the four mounted policemen that always rode at the end of the parade. She wondered where Tony and Tina could be. Surely they wouldn't stay home from the parade.

Finally the last truck rolled by. On it stood the sword swallower. He was not swallowing his sword just then. He was eating peanuts and throwing the shells in the air. Then the mounted policemen rode by. But there was no Tony and no Tina. Betsy and Billy were terribly disappointed.

"Well, where were your friends?" said Kenny.

"I don't know," said Billy. "It's awful funny."

"Sure it's funny," said Kenny. "Didn't I say they made it up, Chris?"

"I knew they made it up all the time," said Christopher.

"Well, it's awful funny," said Billy.

Betsy whispered to Billy on the way back to the room. "Maybe it wasn't true what Tony and Tina told us. Maybe they made it all up."

"If they did," said Billy, "it's a mean trick."

Billy had been daydreaming about getting acquainted with five elephants, three trained seals, and six poodles, and now his daydream had fallen apart. He felt cheated.

"I'm going over to the circus grounds this afternoon," said Billy. "I'm going to find out about them."

"How?" said Betsy.

"I'll find the trailer they said they live in

and I'll go right up and knock on the door
and ask if they live there."

"Oh, you'd be scared to do that," said
Betsy.

"No, I wouldn't," Billy replied.

"Well, I'll ask my mother if I can go with
you," said Betsy.

"Okay," said Billy.

As Betsy and Billy walked home from
school, Betsy said, "How'll we get over to the
circus grounds? It's awfully far."

"We can go on the bus," said Billy.

"Do you know how to go on the bus?"
Betsy asked.

"My mother will tell me," said Billy.

When the children parted, Billy said, "So
long, Betsy. I'll call you up and tell you where
to meet me."

"All right," said Betsy.

When Billy reached his house he found his
mother working in the garden. "Mother," said
Billy, "you know those circus kids I told you
about that Betsy and I met yesterday?" His
mother looked up. "Well," Billy continued,
"they weren't in the parade. Betsy and I are
going over to where the circus is and see if
they really do live in that trailer and have all

those animals and a mother who's a bareback rider and everything."

"You are not going to the circus grounds with Betsy," said his mother.

"Why not?" said Billy. "I can find it on the bus."

"I wouldn't think of letting you go and I'm sure that Betsy's mother won't let her go," said Mrs. Porter.

"Aw, Mother," said Billy. "How am I going to find out about Tony and Tina if I can't go look for them?"

"You don't need to look for them," said his mother. "They were probably just two children making up a lot of nonsense, and you and Betsy believed it. Now just forget about it."

"But, Mother, maybe it was true. Maybe their father does have elephants and seals and poodles. Maybe Tony and Tina couldn't be in the parade this morning. Maybe they had measles or something."

"Well, if they have measles, you certainly can't go to see them," said his mother.

"Well, I don't really think they have the measles," said Billy. "Maybe they have a baby brother or something and they had to mind the baby while their father and mother went in the parade."

"Billy," said his mother, "you cannot go to the circus grounds and I don't want to hear another word about it."

"Oh, *Mother!*" said Billy, as he went inside to telephone to Betsy. When Betsy answered the telephone, Billy said, "Betsy, my mother won't let me go over to the circus."

"Mine won't let me go either," said Betsy. "My mother thinks they just made it up."

"So does mine," replied Billy. "But my father's going to take me to see the circus next Saturday and then I'm going to try to find out about Tony and Tina."

"My father's going to take me, too," said Betsy. "Maybe then we can ask the animal trainer or maybe the merry-go-round man."

"Yes, maybe," said Billy.

"I'll see you tomorrow in school," said Betsy.

"So long," replied Billy. "Be seeing you."

The next morning, shortly after school had begun, the door of Betsy's classroom opened. Betsy looked up, and there in the doorway stood Tony and Tina. Miss Brown, the principal, was with them.

"Go in," said Miss Brown, to the two children. Tony and Tina entered the room. "Miss Ross," said Miss Brown, "here are two new children for you. They are Tina and Tony." Miss Ross shook hands with the two children. "It is very late in the term for these children to enter the class," the principal said, "but their father and mother are with the circus, and the circus is going to South America. The children are staying here with their aunt."

"Have they been to school before?" asked Miss Ross.

"No," replied Miss Brown. "Their mother has taught them. But I gave them tests yesterday and I find that they are ready for this grade."

Billy was looking all around the room and grinning from ear to ear. Then he leaned over Kenny's shoulder and said, "They're my friends. That's Tony that I told you about. His father has elephants and seals and poodle dogs and his mother is a bareback rider and he's my friend."

Miss Brown went out of the room and closed the door.

"Miss Ross," said Betsy, "Tina is a friend of mine."

"And Tony's a friend of mine," said Billy.

Tina's and Tony's faces lighted up as they looked at Miss Ross and nodded their heads. "That's right," said Tony.

Miss Ross placed Tina at an empty desk near Betsy, and Tony she placed near Billy. "Hello, Tony!" said Billy.

"Hello!" said Tony.

Billy leaned over Kenny's shoulder again. "His uncle owns the merry-go-round. What do you know about that!"

Betsy looked back at Billy. Her face was one large grin. Billy winked his eye.

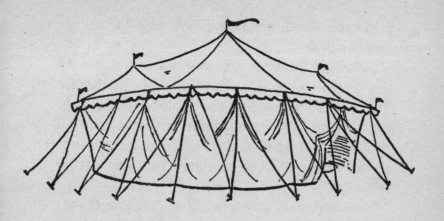

CHAPTER 8
An Invitation

Tony and Tina were the pride of Betsy's class. The children went among the rest of the boys and girls in the school saying, "Did you know that we have a boy and girl in our room whose father and mother are in the circus? Their father has five elephants and three trained seals and six poodle dogs that do tricks." The whole school was impressed. Wherever the twins went, a crowd followed them. Betsy and Billy felt very im-

113

portant indeed, because Tony and Tina were their friends.

Betsy walked around the schoolyard with her arm around Tina's waist. At lunchtime Betsy saved a place at the table in the lunchroom where she and Ellen always sat. All the girls in the class tried to get places at the same table, now that Tina was sitting there.

On Wednesday, when Ellen came with her tray, all of the seats at the table were filled and Tina was sitting next to Betsy. No one noticed Ellen, not even Betsy. Everyone was busy asking Tina questions about the circus. Ellen carried her tray as far away as possible from the chattering girls. She ate her lunch quickly and went back to her classroom.

As for Tony, Billy was at his side all the time. In the lunchroom Billy always saved a seat next to him for Tony. On Monday he was able to defend Tony's place while Tony got his tray at the lunch counter by yelling, "Hey! Who do you think you are? Get out! That's Tony's place."

But the next day Kenny put his tray on the table.

"Get out of there, Ken!" said Billy.

"Who do you think you are?" said Kenny. "I can sit wherever I please."

"You can't sit there," said Billy. "That's Tony's place."

"It's Tony's place! It's Tony's place!" Kenny sang out. "You think you own Tony, don't you?" And with this Kenny took his glass of milk from the tray and placed it on the table.

Billy jumped up. "Well, you didn't even believe he was real," he said, and gave Kenny a shove. Kenny was standing on one foot. He lost his balance and toppled over. As he fell his hand struck the edge of his tray. The tray flipped over and Kenny landed on the floor in a shower of crackers, cookies, hard-boiled eggs, sliced ham, and whole-wheat bread.

While Kenny was picking himself up, Tony slid into the chair at the table. Kenny was furious. He got up and, without looking, swung his fist in the direction of Billy. But he did not hit anything, because Billy had fled to the lunch counter, where he was very busy talking to Mrs. Tipple, the woman who was in charge.

"Which do you think is the best, the chocolate pudding or the Jell-O?" said Billy.

Kenny rushed up to the counter. "He knocked me over," he cried, "and all my lunch is spoiled. It's all on the floor."

"That's just too bad," said Mrs. Tipple. "Stay away from trouble, Kenny, and you won't get into it." She picked up a sandwich. "Here!" she said. "Take this sandwich and remember that you're a mighty lucky boy to get another one."

Kenny took it and murmured, "Thank you."

Then he picked up the lunch and the tray from the floor. All the time he was mutter-

ing, "I'm never going to have anything to do with you fellows again. Never! I wouldn't care if you owned the whole circus. I wouldn't look at your old circus. Not if you paid me a million dollars. Not if you paid me ten million dollars."

Billy and Tony calmly ate their lunch.

By this time Kenny had cleared up the floor. He picked up his glass of milk and sat down in the farthest corner of the room. There he ate his sandwich and drank his milk, muttering to himself.

On Thursday morning, when the twins arrived at school, they went right to Miss Ross. Tony said something to the teacher and Tina nodded her head.

"Why, how very nice!" Betsy heard Miss Ross say. "Shall I tell the boys and girls?"

"Yes, please," said Tony.

As soon as the bell rang for school to begin, Miss Ross said, "Boys and girls, I have some wonderful news for you." Every face in the room turned toward Miss Ross. You could have heard a pin drop. "Tony and Tina have asked me to tell you that the whole class is invited to attend the Saturday afternoon performance of the circus."

"Whee!" the children exclaimed.

"For free?" said Kenny.

"Yes," said Miss Ross. "It's free."

"How'll we get there?" asked Mary Lou.

"Oh, Miss Ross," said Tony, "I forgot to tell you. My father said he would send one of the trucks over to pick everybody up. He says he can put some benches inside."

"That will be very nice," said Miss Ross. "Everyone who wishes to go will please be at the schoolyard gate at half past one."

"Are you going too, Miss Ross?" said Betsy.

"Yes, indeed," replied Miss Ross. "I wouldn't miss it for anything. Tonight you must ask your parents if you may go. Be sure to let me know tomorrow, so that Tony's father will know how many seats to save."

The children were so excited they could talk of nothing else the rest of the day. Kenny forgot all about how mad he was at Billy and Tony. He kept saying, "It sure is swell! Imagine, we're going to the circus free!" Later he said, "Hi, Tony! Will we sit right down front?"

"Sure," said Tony.

"And maybe the clowns will talk to us?" Kenny asked. "Do you think they will, maybe?"

"Of course," said Tony. "They're my friends. They'll all talk to you."

"That's swell," said Kenny.

Everybody in the class was happy except Ellen. Everyone's face was smiling, but not Ellen's. Yesterday she had rushed right out of school the minute the bell rang. She did the same thing today.

Betsy's mother came with the car, to pick up Betsy. She found Betsy and Billy, Tony and Tina, in a tight bunch by the schoolyard gate. They all seemed to be talking at once. Of course they were talking about the circus. Betsy's mother blew the horn and the children jumped.

"Oh, there's Mother," said Betsy. "Come along, Billy. Come along, Tina and Tony. Mother will take you home."

The four children ran to the car. "Mother," said Betsy, "this is Tina and this is Tony. You'll drive them home, won't you?"

Mother said, "How do you do, Tina. How do you do, Tony. I have heard a lot about you. Hop in." Tina and Tony both said how-do-you-do, and hopped into the back of the car.

Betsy and Billy got into the front seat. Betsy's mother turned to the children on the back seat. "Where do you want me to take you?" she asked. "Are you still living at the circus?"

"No," replied Tony, "we're living with our aunt now on Hicks Street. Mama wanted us to get used to it before she and Papa left with the circus."

"Can you tell me how to get to Hicks Street?" said Betsy's mother. "I am afraid I don't know where it is."

Betsy spoke up. "It isn't very far from Ellen's, Mother. Just drive over toward Ellen's."

Her mother started the car. "By the way," she said, "where *is* Ellen?"

"I don't know," said Betsy. "She must have gone right home from school."

"She did," said Billy. "I saw her running up the street."

"Oh, Mother," exclaimed Betsy. "I have such exciting news."

"You bet!" said Billy.

"What is it?" Mother asked.

"We're all going to the circus on Saturday afternoon," said Betsy. "The whole class! And it's free!"

"Tony's father has invited us," said Billy.

"Isn't that wonderful!" said Betsy's mother.

"And we're going in a circus truck," said Betsy.

"Is Miss Ross going too?" Mother asked.

"Yes, Miss Ross is going," replied Betsy. "I can go, can't I, Mother?"

"Of course. If Miss Ross is going, you can go," said Mother. "I thought you had a date to go with Father."

"Oh, my father was going to take me, too," said Billy, "but I'd rather go with the class."

"So would I," said Betsy, "in the circus truck."

"Now I am almost to Ellen's house," said Mother. "You will have to tell me where to turn."

"At the next corner," said Tony.

Mother turned the car into Hicks Street. The street was narrow and the houses were very small and quite old, but some had fresh paint and looked very cozy.

"It's down near the end of the block," said Tony.

The car went slowly toward the end of the block. Then Tony called out, "Here it is!" He pointed to a house that looked even older than the other houses, because almost all the paint had peeled off of it. Betsy's mother stopped the car.

"My aunt works," said Tony, "so she isn't home. But I have the key in my pocket." Tony fished in his pocket for the key. When he found it, the twins stepped out of the car.

"Thanks a lot," said Tony.

"Thank you," said Tina.

"You're quite welcome," said Betsy's mother.

As the car started, Betsy called out, "Goodby!" Billy called, "See you tomorrow!" The twins waved and the car drove off.

Tony put the key in the lock while Tina waited on the front step. "I hate this house," said Tina. "It's ugly. Everything in the circus is pretty, bright colors and pretty pictures all over. And our trailer has curtains at the windows."

Tony opened the front door and the children went into a dark hall. A piece of the ceiling paper had come loose and hung down from the ceiling. The draft from the open door blew the paper and made it flap. Tina jumped. "I don't want to stay here," she said. "I want to go with Mama and Papa and the circus." She began to cry.

"Well, you can't go," said Tony. "We have

to wait here until they come back." Then he said, "I'm hungry. Let's see if there's something to eat."

The children went into the kitchen. A jar of peanut butter stood on the table beside a loaf of bread. Tony made himself a sandwich, picked up his ball, and ran out to play.

Tina stood looking out of the front window as she ate her sandwich. There was such a big lump in her throat she could hardly swallow. Tony had disappeared with his ball. She guessed he had found someone to play with. Tina wished that she had someone to play with. She pressed her nose against the windowpane and tears rolled down her cheeks.

Then she saw a little girl about her own age coming down the street on the opposite side. She had a jumping rope. Tina watched as she came nearer. And suddenly her heart gave a little leap, for it was someone she knew. It was Ellen. Tina rushed out into the little hall, pulled open the front door, and ran across the street calling, "Ellen! Ellen!"

Ellen stood still and looked at Tina, but only for a moment. Then she turned and ran away.

Tina went slowly back to the house. She

walked up to the front door. It was locked. In her hurry to go to meet Ellen she had forgotten to take the key. She sat down on the step and cried until she could cry no longer. She simply ran out of tears.

At last she saw Aunt Millie coming down the street. Tony ran by her side, talking and laughing. And there's nothing to laugh about, thought Tina. Nothing at all.

CHAPTER 9

The Drive to the Circus

On Friday morning the children came to school shouting to each other, "I can go to the circus." One after another came bouncing into the classroom saying, "My mother says I can go to the circus tomorrow."

When the bell rang for school to begin, Miss Ross said, "Well, it looks as though everyone is going to the circus." She looked around the room. "Is there anyone who is not going with us tomorrow?" Ellen raised

126

her hand. "Oh, Ellen," said Miss Ross, "that's too bad. Why can't you go?"

"I don't like the circus," said Ellen, in a very stiff voice.

"Oh!" exclaimed the children.

"She doesn't like the circus!" said Kenny.

"She must be crazy!" said Christopher.

Ellen looked as though she were going to cry. "Now," said Miss Ross, "we'll have no more remarks like that, Christopher. Ellen, no doubt, has a good reason."

Betsy thought it was very strange. She wondered what was the matter with Ellen. At recess she waited for Ellen in the schoolyard, by the door, but Ellen did not come out. Instead, she sat at her desk and read a book. When the class went to the lunchroom at twelve o'clock, all the girls scrambled for places near Tina and Betsy—all but Ellen.

Tina sat beside Betsy, and Mary Lou rushed to the seat on the other side of Betsy. "I'm sorry, Mary Lou," said Betsy, "but I am saving that seat for Ellen."

"Oh, all right," said Mary Lou. She moved to the other side of the table.

Betsy kept watching the door for Ellen. She began to wonder what was keeping her upstairs so long. Finally she decided to go look for her. She went up to the classroom. Miss Ross was writing the spelling words on the blackboard. When she saw Betsy she said, "Did you want something, Betsy?"

"I'm looking for Ellen," said Betsy. "She hasn't come to lunch yet."

"Oh, Ellen has gone home," said Miss Ross. "She was excused for the afternoon. Her mother is taking her to the dentist's."

"Oh!" said Betsy. She turned and went back to finish her lunch.

After school Betsy went home with Billy Porter. Her mother had taken Star to the city to get new shoes, so Mrs. Porter had said that Betsy could play with Billy and stay for supper. The two children played checkers most of the afternoon. They had been keeping a score ever since Christmas, and the score had been tied for three weeks. Each one was trying hard to get ahead of the other. By the time supper was ready Betsy was ahead by one game. As Billy gathered up the checkers he said, "Just wait! I'll beat you next time."

After supper Mr. Porter drove Betsy home, and it was not until Betsy was in bed that she thought again of Ellen. She wondered why Ellen didn't want to go to the circus. She didn't believe that Ellen didn't like the circus. But soon she fell asleep. The following morning, when Betsy woke up, she was so excited about going to the circus that she didn't think of Ellen at all.

Long before half past one, the children in Betsy's class were gathered together at the schoolyard gate. The boys were wrestling, grabbing each other's hats, and chasing each other. The girls were in little bunches, chattering like magpies. At last Miss Ross arrived. She was wearing her best coat and hat, and the girls all rushed up to her and stood admiring her clothes.

"My mother has a coat like that," said Mary Lou. "Only it's green and it has a double row of buttons and the collar is bigger and she doesn't have any cuffs. My mother's coat is much fuller, but it's got exactly the same kind of pockets."

Mary Lou was cut short by a shout from the boys. "Here comes the truck! Here comes the circus truck!"

"But Tony and Tina aren't here yet," said Betsy.

"Where do you suppose they are?" said Billy.

All the children were watching the truck as it came nearer. Suddenly Kenny cried out, "There are Tony and Tina in the truck."

Sure enough, the twins were riding on the seat beside the driver. They were waving to the waiting crowd. All the children waved back. The truck drew up at the curb and stopped.

The children looked at it with open mouths. The first surprise was the driver. He was a circus clown. Then the truck! It was the most magnificent truck they had ever seen. It was painted bright pink and it had a gold roof. The spokes of the wheels were gold. Right on the side of the truck, surrounded by gold curlicues, was a picture of a huge lion and a man. The man was wearing a beautiful tight purple jacket and bright blue tights. There were large black letters under the picture which the children read aloud. *Baron Mitzki, the World's Most Daring Lion Tamer.*

The clown jumped down from the driver's seat, ran around to the back of the truck, and whipped out a ladder. "Come along," he said. "In you go!"

The children were speechless as they climbed into the back of the truck. The boys clambered right in, but the clown took hold of each little girl's hand. As he grasped Betsy's she thought, This is the first time I ever touched a real, live clown! She was sure that his hand felt quite different from other people's.

Miss Ross was the last to get into the truck. "Sit right down," she said to the children, and they scrambled for seats. They all wanted to be as close to the driver as possible.

The clown closed up the back of the truck with a great rattle of chains, and in a moment there was a lurch and the truck started.

Suddenly all the children shouted. They did not all shout the same thing, but it all meant the same thing—*Hurray!*

"Children," said Miss Ross, "you must be quiet. You cannot shout, even though you are going to the circus."

"Miss Ross," said Betsy, "isn't it a beautiful truck? I feel as though I were part of the circus, don't you?"

"I certainly do, Betsy," replied Miss Ross.

As the gay truck rolled through the streets, everyone stopped to look at it. "I guess everybody thinks we *are* in the circus," said Mary Lou.

"I'm sure they do," said Miss Ross.

"It's wonderful!" said Sally Jane.

Kenny began to let out great roars. "I'm the lion," he said, opening his mouth very wide and clawing the air. He got up off the bench and began to claw Christopher, who was sitting opposite him.

"Sit down, Kenny," said Miss Ross. "You may be the lion, but I am the lion tamer, so sit down."

All the children laughed and Kenny sat down. Billy was hanging over the back of the driver's seat. Suddenly he turned around and shouted, "I can see the circus grounds! We're getting near. I can see the flags on the big tent."

All the children stood up and tried to see out of the front of the truck. "Sit down," said Miss Ross, "before you fall down." The children sat down. Now they could hear the music of the merry-go-round. Betsy began to feel tingly all over. She always felt tingly when she was excited.

The truck was moving slowly now, for they were driving through the circus grounds. Outside, everyone was shouting different things. "Buy a balloon! Buy a balloon!" "Here you are! Get your candy cotton!" "Ladies and gentlemen, the fattest lady in the world! She weighs five hundred and sixty pounds!" "Step right up! Step right up and see Princess Rama, the snake charmer." "Hot dogs! Hot dogs!" "Lemonade! Lemonade! Get a glass of ice-cold lemonade!" And then the voice of a little boy screaming, "I lost my yellow balloon!"

Honk! Honk! went the horn on the truck. Honk! Honk!

Then the children could hear other voices. "Oh, look at the circus wagon!" "Look at the clown, driving the circus truck!" "What do you suppose is in the circus truck?" "Why, it's full of children!" The children in the truck had never felt so important. At last the truck came to a stop. It stopped at a side entrance of the big tent.

Tony, Tina, and the driver jumped down. They came around to the back of the truck and put up the ladder. The children formed in line to wait their turn to go down.

There, waiting to meet them, stood three more clowns and the beautiful bareback rider. One of the clowns was holding a big bunch of balloons. As the children came down the ladder, he handed each one a balloon.

Tina was holding tightly to the hand of the

beautiful bareback rider. "This is my mother," she kept saying. Her mother shook hands with each one of the children in turn.

When she shook hands with Kenny he said, "You sure are pretty. I didn't know that bareback riders were mothers." Tina's mother laughed and this made her prettier than ever.

Tony was busy introducing the clowns. "This is Pogo," he said. "This is Butterscotch!"

Billy thought Butterscotch was a wonderful name for a clown.

"And this is Toto," said Tony.

The driver of the truck turned out to have the best name of all. It was Lollipop!

Each clown gathered a small group of children together and led them through the door into the big tent. Miss Ross brought up the rear. Betsy was amazed to see how big the tent was inside. It went up and up and up into three high points. Row upon row of benches rose high around the sides of the tent. They were filled with people who were making a great deal of noise, for they were all talking and laughing. Many of the children in the seats clapped their hands when they saw the clowns.

Betsy and Billy were both with Lollipop.

He had each one by the hand. They led the whole class.

Finally the long parade of children with the clowns reached the empty benches that were being saved especially for them. They climbed into their seats and settled themselves.

Mary Lou had just sat down when she let go of her balloon. Up it went! Every face in the whole tent was turned up, watching the balloon as it grew smaller and smaller until it reached the highest point of the tent. There it bumped itself and came to a stop.

"It doesn't look any bigger than a red lollipop now," Betty Jane called out.

Lollipop, the clown, looked up at the balloon and said, "Who? Me?"

This made the children laugh.

Suddenly a horn blew. An opening in the opposite side of the tent appeared and the magnificent circus parade entered. The show had begun!

CHAPTER 10
Ellen and Tina

On Monday morning, when the children arrived at school, they were still excited about the circus that they had seen on Saturday.

"I wish we were going to see it all over again next Saturday," said Billy.

"It's all over now," said Kenny. "The circus left this morning."

When Tina and Tony arrived they did not look very happy, for they had just said good-by to their mother and father. All the questions and chatter about the circus, however, helped them to forget their sorrow.

When Ellen arrived, Kenny called out, "Oh, Ellen, you missed it!"

"Oh, yes," said Mary Lou, "it was wonderful."

Ellen made no reply. Betsy went up to Ellen and said, "Ellen, why didn't you go with us to the circus?"

"I went to a party," said Ellen.

"Oh," said Betsy, "whose party?"

"My best friend's," said Ellen.

"Oh," said Betsy, "who is she?"

"Marjorie," said Ellen.

"Marjorie?" repeated Betsy. And at that moment the bell rang.

"Take your seat, Betsy," said Miss Ross.

Marjorie, thought Betsy, as she walked to her seat. She had never heard of Marjorie. She didn't know any Marjorie. Suddenly Betsy felt unhappy, as though a cloud had settled down over her. At recess time Betsy caught hold of Ellen. "Ellen," she said, "where does your friend Marjorie live?"

"Near me," said Ellen.

"Where does she go to school?" Betsy asked.

"She goes to private school," said Ellen.

"Oh!" said Betsy.

"And she goes to dancing school," said Ellen. "And she has beautiful dresses—hundreds
of them. And pink slippers." With this, Ellen
ran off.

Betsy spent the rest of her recess time with
Tina, but she kept thinking about Ellen's
friend Marjorie. She did not save a place for
Ellen at the table in the lunchroom. She hardly
noticed when Mary Lou sat down on one side
of her and Tina on the other.

Betsy ate her sandwich and stared across
the room at the back of Ellen's curly red
head. The talking in the lunchroom went on
around her, but she didn't hear it. She was
busy with her own thoughts. She walked
home from school alone. When she reached
her house she found her mother in the garden. She was putting some little plants along
the edge of the flower bed. The bed was full
of tulips, purple and pink and white. They
were like delicate china cups held up to the
sun.

"Hello, Betsy," said Mother, when she saw
Betsy coming toward her.

"Hello," said Betsy.

Mother put her arm around Betsy and

looked down at her. "You don't look like Mother's sunshine this afternoon."

"Mother," said Betsy, "Ellen has a new best friend. Her name is Marjorie and she goes to private school."

"Is that so?" said her mother. "Does that make you unhappy?"

Betsy nodded her head. Mother looked at the garden. "Aren't the tulips beautiful?" she said.

"Yes," said Betsy.

"Suppose I only had one tulip in my garden," said her mother. "The garden wouldn't be nearly so pretty, would it?"

"No," said Betsy.

"And they are all different," said Mother. "Come and see." Mother pointed to the tulips. Each one was a little bit different from all the others. "But they are all important, dear," said her mother. "They all help to make the garden lovely."

"Yes," said Betsy.

"You see, darling," said Mother, "we each have a garden in our hearts, where our friendships grow. Each one is different but each one is important."

"Mother," said Betsy, pointing to a large

white tulip with ruffly pink edges, "that's the biggest tulip of all and it's the prettiest."

"Yes, it is, dear," said Mother. "But it doesn't take anything away from all the other tulips. It just makes the garden more beautiful."

Betsy began to feel a little bit happier.

"Betsy," said her mother, "perhaps Ellen feels that your new friend Tina has crowded her out of your garden."

Betsy looked surprised. She looked up into her mother's face and said, "Oh, do you think she does?"

"That may be the reason why Ellen didn't go to the circus on Saturday," said Mother.

"Oh, no, Mother," said Betsy. "Ellen said she went to Marjorie's party."

"Did she?" said Mother. "Perhaps Ellen would like to come and spend the night with you next Friday."

"I'll ask her," said Betsy.

Next day Betsy met Ellen as she was walking to school. Linda and a bunch of kindergarten children were strung out like a long tail behind Ellen.

"Hello, Ellen," said Betsy.

"Hello," said Ellen.

"How is Marjorie?" said Betsy.

"She's very well," replied Ellen.

"Can you come and spend the night with me on Friday?" Betsy asked.

"Why don't you ask Tina?" said Ellen.

"Because I want you," said Betsy. "Ellen, Mother told me all about it yesterday. You have a garden."

"Who has a garden?" said Ellen.

"Everybody has a garden," replied Betsy. "Not in the yard, in your heart."

"Oh!" said Ellen.

"And all your friends are tulips," said Betsy.

"Why are they tulips?" Ellen asked.

"Well, they don't have to be tulips," said Betsy. "They can be any kind of flowers— just make-believe! I like to make believe that they're tulips."

"I would like roses best," said Ellen.

"All right," said Betsy. "Well, if you only had one rose, it would be pretty, but it wouldn't be as nice as a lot of roses."

Ellen thought about this and then she said, "No, it wouldn't."

"Well," said Betsy, "when you have a lot of friends it's nicer, too."

"Oh!" said Ellen.

"But, Ellen," said Betsy, "you're the nicest tulip. You're my best one."

Ellen smiled, and it was a very sunny smile. "Am I?" she said.

"Oh, yes!" said Betsy.

"I would like to be a rose," said Ellen. "Couldn't I be a rose?"

"Okay," said Betsy.

At lunchtime Betsy sat between Tina and Ellen. Betsy and Ellen did the talking. Tina was very quiet. Once or twice Ellen glanced at Tina.

After school Ellen took her jumping rope and went down the street and around the block until she reached Hicks Street. She skipped rope along the sidewalk. After a while she stopped and looked across the street. There, sitting on a step, was Tina. She was bent over with her head on her arm and she was crying. Ellen ran across the street. She sat down on the step beside Tina. "What's the matter, Tina?" she asked.

"Tony's gone to play at Billy Porter's house," said Tina, "and I'm scared to go in the house, 'cause of the wallpaper."

Ellen put her arm around Tina and said, "Don't cry, Tina."

Tina cried harder. "I want my Mama!" she said.

"Come on over to my house," said Ellen, standing up. "Mummy is home."

Tina got up and the two little girls walked slowly back to Ellen's house. Ellen's mother

gave them each a cup of cocoa and a big sugar cookie. They played with Ellen's dolls until Tina said, "I guess I better go home now. I guess my Aunt Millie will be home soon."

"I'll walk home with you," said Ellen. "And I'll go in the house with you, so you won't be afraid of the wallpaper."

"Oh, that's nice!" said Tina.

Tina and Ellen walked back to Tina's house. Just as they got there, Tina's aunt opened the front door. "Hello, Tina," she said. "I came out to look for you."

"Aunt Millie," said Tina, "this is my friend Ellen."

"Hello, Ellen," said Aunt Millie. "Won't you come in?"

"No, thank you," said Ellen. "I have to go home for my dinner now."

"Good-by, Ellen," said Tina. "I liked it at your house."

"Good-by," said Ellen. "Please come again. Come any time."

When Tina was setting the table, Aunt Millie said, "Did you have a good time at Ellen's, Tina?"

"Oh, yes," replied Tina. "Ellen likes to make believe. She says she's a rose in a garden."

"Is that so?" said her aunt.

"Yes. And she says I am a rose, too," said Tina.

On Friday Ellen went home with Betsy.

She had her toothbrush and her comb and brush and nightie in a little bag. After dinner Star and Betsy and Ellen played a game until it was time to go to bed. While Betsy and Ellen were getting undressed, Betsy said, "How is Marjorie, Ellen?"

Ellen hesitated for a moment. Then she said, "She's all right."

"Have you seen her this week?" Betsy asked.

"Not this week," replied Ellen.

"Does she really have hundreds of dresses?"

"Well, not hundreds," said Ellen.

After the two girls were tucked into bed and the light was out, Ellen said, "Betsy!"

"What?" said Betsy.

"It's about Marjorie," said Ellen.

"What about her?" said Betsy.

"Well," said Ellen, "she isn't real. She's just a make-believe friend."

Betsy sat up in bed. "But you said she had a party last Saturday," said Betsy.

"I just made believe she had a party," said Ellen.

"Oh, Ellen," said Betsy, "do you mean you told a lie?"

"Well, not exactly," said Ellen. "I got my little dishes out and I set the table and I had cookies and I made believe Marjorie was there."

"But that wasn't Marjorie's party," said Betsy. "That was your party."

"No, it wasn't," said Ellen, "because I was making believe it was Marjorie's party."

"Ellen," said Betsy, "it's terrible to tell things that aren't true."

"But I didn't," said Ellen. "Marjorie is my real make-believe friend."

"You mean you still have her?" said Betsy.

"Of course," said Ellen.

"Oh! Well then, that's all right," said Betsy.

And soon they were both asleep.

Take Betsy home with you!
The Betsy Books

by Carolyn Haywood

Every day's an adventure with Betsy, her little sister Star, and all their friends from the long-time favorite series. Don't miss a single wonderful story!

___BETSY AND THE CIRCUS 40197-6 $3.25
___BETSY'S BUSY SUMMER 40171-2 $3.25
___BETSY'S LITTLE STAR 40172-0 $3.25